MAROONED *on* PLANET ANDROID

MORE BY THE AUTHOR

Planet Android series:

Mysteries of Planet Android

Standalone:

Goddess Found

MAROONED *on* PLANET ANDROID

Planet Android Book 1

CALANTHE COLT

CENTAURI PUBLISHING

This novel is entirely a work of fiction. The names, characters, and incidents portrayed in it are the work of the author's imagination. Any resemblance to actual persons, living or dead; events; or localities is entirely coincidental.

Published by Centauri Publishing.

ISBN (paperback): 978-0-473-70393-6
ISBN (Kindle): 978-0-473-70395-0
ISBN (generic ePub): 978-0-473-70394-3

A catalogue record of this book is available from the National Library of New Zealand Te Puna Mātauranga o Aotearoa.

To everyone who didn't know until they grew up that most people consider sci fi to be a 'boy' thing, because it certainly wasn't in their household.

CHAPTER 1

Marcie wished she hadn't checked the mail from home until after her shift.

She scrubbed the tears from her face with the back of her hand. Before she could second-guess herself, she tore down the Martian holiday print of her and Lisa from her message board. After everything, how could she do this to Marcie? Break up with her while she was on a mission, months out from Sol? A mission into deadspace where they would only get intermittent communication? Lisa knew Marcie would only get mail from home sporadically.

But it was probably time, after all. None of her relationships lasted long after her partners realised how much time she spent out on missions. Apparently Marcie just wasn't worth the effort.

The mail from Lisa arrived at the same time as one from her parents in the Midlands, dated a week later, saying they had all her stuff back from London. Oh, and

Lisa had a girlfriend—a corporate lawyer. It was all done and dusted before she'd even heard about it.

She took a deep breath and looked out the porthole. The view outside was darker than normal, a deep black that simply couldn't be seen from Sol, not even at the heliopause. The *Sunda Tiger* had left the Orion Spur far behind and was ploughing its way into the emptier space on the way to the Perseus Arm. There were still stars out here, and the Milky Way was still visible around them, of course. But there were far fewer bright magnitude stars nearby than there were near Earth. Everything was so far away. Sometimes it felt to Marcie like she could see the heat death of the universe in action out here between the galaxy's arms.

Marcie pulled out the sink drawer and washed her face, hoping to get rid of the puffiness before her shift. Some water splashed to the outer edge of her cabin, the part that protruded beyond the gravity web because of the hull's outward curvature. The water droplets floated in her weird little pocket of zero-g. She didn't have time to scoop it back to gravity. She knew from experience it'd make it back over the gravity web to fall on the floor by itself eventually. Instead, she jammed herself into her white jumpsuit with the orange engineering section piping, shoved a tooth-cleaning capsule in her mouth and ran along the corridor, scraping her dark pixie-cut hair into a semblance of order with her fingers. She had less than five minutes to get up two decks and along 200m of bright white and grey corridors to her station at the rear of the ship.

Marcie zipped through the door, her boots clanking on the thinly plasticised metal decking, and into her work station mere moments before her shift began. The energising scent of ozone and warm machinery surrounded her. She hoped no one would take any notice of her, shadowed as she was under one of the great magnetic bottle cooling tubes. But it seemed her bad luck hadn't ended for the day.

"Lieutenant Martin-Palmer! So good of you to join us!" said Lieutenant Commander Simons, Head of Engineering. He rested his hands on a safety rail above her workstation and stared at her, the red light of a security sign behind him turning his perfectly coiffed blond-ish hair into an ominous halo.

Marcie winced. Tyler Simons was her least favourite person on the *Sunda Tiger*. He was big, brash, and American, his chiselled jaw *just so perfect* it was no doubt enhanced. He had a politician father who 'encouraged' the Orion Navy to promote Simons to Head Engineer. He knew engineering, sure, but he didn't know leadership. Not to mention that he spent far too much time at his desk reading his personal mails and whatnot, i.e. what the rest of them did off duty. And, for some reason, he'd shoulder-tapped Marcie to be his 2IC for the mission. It wasn't because she'd earned it: she wasn't any better than the others who had shared her status before her promotion.

Marcie pointed to the time read-out on her panel. "I'm on time, sir." She turned to her station and pulled up the Weft-Skip schedule for the day. They would do four skips that day — a crushing schedule with the engine downtime needed between each one. They were on a long-range mission and no one wanted it to take too long. It was also an important day for the mission: after the second skip, they would be in range of any subspace relays still operational around the missing colony 227C. By the middle of the day, they might be in contact with anyone who still lived there and still had operational tech.

"It's good manners to be here five minutes early for social bonding time, lieutenant," Simons said from above and behind her, breaking her concentration.

Marcie ignored him and applied herself to her work. She wouldn't have minded social time with the rest of the five engineers rostered on. It was just Simons she avoided.

When Simons recommended Marcie's promotion, her first assumption had been that it was because her mother had been a well-regarded engineer for Sol Corp before Marcie was born, but Simons didn't seem to know or care about that. Her next suspicion was racism, because she considered both Sandeep, an Indian, and Ife, a Nigerian, to be more qualified than her, and Simons was exactly the sort of person to be racist. She wasn't sure if she was more relieved or horrified when Ife had a quiet word with her and told her it was because it was her job to crawl into the access hatches in the zero-g annex that buffered the Antimatter Insertion Point before and after each skip, and that Simons stared at her arse while she did so. Gross. She'd seen him staring at Ife's arse too occasionally, so maybe he *was* an equal-opportunity sleaze.

"Are you all right, Marcie?" a quiet voice asked. Sandeep stood nearby, reading from a tablet, but looking at her out of the corner of his eye. "You look puffy round the eyes."

Marcie smiled at him. What a mother hen. "I'm fine."

"Bad mail from home?"

Marcie shrugged. "No one's hurt, so not that bad." Most news wasn't that bad anymore since the end of the Orion War, when Marcie was a small child. Her parents still feared checking their mail in a way that creeped Marcie out whenever she thought of it. Being dumped was better than yet another mail about a dead cousin or school friend or old Sol Corp colleague. Still hurt like an unexpected high-G turn, though.

"Trouble with your girl back home?" It wasn't Sandeep asking this time: it was Simons again. How could such a large man move so quietly? He'd snuck up on them. Marcie tried to keep her face expressionless, but the truth must have been visible. "Dumped, huh? I'm sorry to hear it," said Simons as if she'd answered him, his face sly. "You're bisexual, right? You going to choose a rebound *girl* or a rebound *guy*? Some colony hick? Someone closer to home?"

Pansexual, not bisexual, but even so. Marcie had never, *ever* discussed her sexuality with Simons. How the fuck did he know that? Creep! "I'm going to run the numbers on these Weft-Skips. Sir."

Simons held his hands up. "No need to get your panties in a twist, *lieutenant*. Just makin' conversation." He slapped his hand down on the side of her workstation. "I want those numbers in ten minutes, Lieutenant Martin-Palmer. No dawdling. And those sims too, Lieutenant Chaudhary."

"Aye, sir," both Marcie and Sandeep said in unison. They both let out sighs as Simons stalked off to bother someone else, this time the poor cadet on his second mission who stuttered when he talked.

Ife slid down one of the access ladders and approached them a moment later. "Are you two all right? I was too far off to help."

"Fine," said Marcie. "He was just being himself."

Sandeep nodded. "Yeah. Marcie told him to 'fuck off' in British."

Ife snorted. "At least weaponised Britishness is good for something."

Marcie laughed. When they had first met, Ife's barbs about the colonising history of Marcie's country were tests of her mettle and temperament, but now they were just normal parts of their friendly banter.

Marcie got to work. She had the numbers for Simons in *eight* minutes, and then she headed into the zero-g annex to perform her routine checks before the first

Weft-Skip. The comfort of 0G lifted her mood and buoyed her against even the knowledge that Simons was no doubt perving at her arse as she worked.

The morning passed quickly. She kept busy with the post-skip checklist after the second skip, so for a few minutes she took no notice of the murmuring and whispers circulating the main part of engineering. When she floated back to gravity and planted her feet on the decking again, Ife bustled straight over to her. "What's going on?" asked Marcie.

"We're now in subspace relay range of the colony."

"Oh, yeah! Anything?"

Ife's face was grim. "No response. They've been trying for nearly an hour up in command and there's nothing, not even an automatic pingback."

Marcie's shoulders slumped. "So, they're gone?"

"Maybe. Moved on. Dead. Still there but knocked back to the dark ages? We won't know 'till we get there in three weeks."

Marcie sighed. It had been a long shot. It always was when the Navy sent a ship to reconnect with one of the distant colonies the Orion Alliance worlds had lost contact with during the war. Sometimes they found a settlement of puzzled people who had no idea the war had ended. Sometimes there were ruins and evidence of space pirate attacks. Since Research Station 227C was so far out from Sol, the latter eventuality was far more likely. Still, it was a letdown.

What a terrible day.

CHAPTER 2

As always, booting back up from a recharge cycle triggered The Memory. His own arms, red. His own hands, blackened and charred. Evidence of a hasty human evacuation all around, but no people. Only androids. Like him. Stumbling around, looking for the people. What people? Who are they?

Who am I?

What did I do?

Being allocated a name and designation from a handwritten list found in a building labelled Mayor's Office.

Altair. Welcome host: Welcome Centre.

Stumbling to the repair centre for a new silicone skin so he would have functional hands. Choosing a different colour so he would not see those red arms again.

Except he did. Every single morning, for the last 28 years, 7 months, 14 days.

Altair did not charge in the recharge station of the guest suite like he was supposed to. The suite had been designed for both human and android visitors to Research Centre 227C, in a time when apparently such had been expected, before the Event Horizon of their collective memory. Therefore, the bed in the suite had a recharge attachment. If he 'slept' on the left, he recharged, and then had the privilege of waking up to dappled light on the ceiling, the gently swaying sheer curtains, birdsong. It made him feel... almost alive.

There were no guests to worry about. No one would ever know.

Altair sat up, as he did every morning, and reassured himself that his body was blue, not red, as he did every morning. He rose, padded to the living room, which was outfitted with a kitchen he did not use and a sectional sofa he occasionally did, and waited for a minute as the sluggishness of the recharge cycle dissipated. Just as he felt fully operational, his familiar Hieraaetus, a small pure white eagle android, swooped through the electrofilm window and landed on its perch, its eyes lighting up blue as it began to recharge. "Good morning, Altair. The time is 7:02 am. The high for today will be 22°C. You have received a summons from Sirius. Please meet him in the Mayor's Office at 7:30 am."

Altair had not been summoned to see Sirius for 4 years, 3 months, and 3 days. The topic of that meeting had been Welcome Centre inventory. Altair considered that the chance of today's meeting regarding a similar topic was at least 89%.

"Thank you, Hieraaetus. Please recharge to 100% before joining me today."

Hieraaetus settled further on the perch and curved a wing over its head in a sleeping pose.

When the androids had first awoken from the Event Horizon, they had been networked and able to share knowledge with each other instantaneously. However, the lack of knowledge of what had happened to the colony before the Event Horizon was of grave concern. Their engineers had considered the possibility of a virus transmitted via their network causing their memory loss to be at least 98%. Therefore, the network had been disengaged, and each member of the colony had been assigned an animal familiar to run messages and deliver information.

Hieraaetus had been with Altair since three days after the Event Horizon, fetching data for him, running messages, and performing minor tasks as requested.

Altair stepped out of the suite into the second-floor corridor of the Welcome Centre. The hallway was quiet. Since he had nearly half an hour before he had to report to Mayor Sirius, he descended to the ground floor of the Welcome Centre and exited through a side door to check the centre gardens before the meeting. Once upon a time, all the hosts had taken care of the garden. But now the plantings were well managed and the trees had grown well, needing only occasional care. Altair alone took care of the weeding and pruning of the gardens, which were planted with selections that represented all the continents of Earth.

He pulled up a few new dandelions, went inside to wash his hands — his blue, not at all burned hands — and exited towards the square in the middle of the settlement.

The oak tree in the middle of the square was large, and for the last 14 years grew acorns which dropped every autumn all over the bench seats underneath. Although no records of the early colony days remained, Altair suspected this oak had been the first tree planted deliberately on 227C. All older trees on the planet would have been seeded by the terraforming drones that preceded the first settlement. None of the other androids going about their business stopped to look at it like he did. But then, everyone saw this tree every day.

Why did Altair still stop and wonder with regularity who had planted it, and where had they gone?

He walked around the tree, which currently bore the bright green leaves and small green immature acorns of early summer, and then entered the building in which Mayor Sirius had his office. The mayor himself, a sparkling white android, sat behind his desk.

Sirius had been designated as Mayor of 227C on the master list when the androids had awoken from the Event Horizon. Whoever had chosen him as mayor had chosen well. Sirius had more organisational programming than other androids, and he often made leaps in logic and drew improbable connections between disparate pieces of information, a useful and adaptable skill Altair would have liked to have.

Vega already waited in the office. Vega was Chief of Security. His presence was... intriguing. Vega too had been red-skinned and blackened after the Event Horizon, and of all the androids he bore the most resemblance in facial structure to Altair. They were unaware if the resemblance meant anything, or if it was simply an artefact of the assembly line. Vega, too, had chosen a new skin colour upon repair, a violet purple. Vega would not be present for discussions of inventory. His familiar, a larger eagle than Altair's own with dark feathers, perched on his shoulder and surveyed the room with the small red lights of a security camera in its eyes.

"Thank you for coming," said Sirius once they were both standing before the desk. "I need to speak with both of you about a concerning situation. The long-range sensors that the engineers repaired last year detected an approaching star ship during our night cycle. Its trajectory suggests its origin is Sol."

There was a moment of silence. The news certainly was not unexpected — the humans would want to know what happened to their colony. But Altair had hoped some clue about what had happened to the former humans would arise before more humans arrived.

"Are we sure the vessel is coming from Sol?" asked Vega.

"No," said Sirius. "That trajectory could have been chosen after departure on purpose to fool us. But since we consider the possibility that humans know of the status of our colony to be no more than 5%, the likelihood of such a subterfuge is also low. The exact likelihood of this ship bearing humans sent to check on the Research Centre 227C colonists is hard to calculate because of many unknown factors."

"Human colonists," said Altair. "Our presence and the lack of humans would be unexpected. And we have no explanation to offer."

Another long pause.

"Yes," said Sirius. "That is a concern. Humans fill in knowledge gaps with fear and distrust. We cannot speak to them before they arrive to apprise them of the situation, as we still have not regained contact with the communications satellites still in orbit."

Whatever event had led to the androids of 227C not remembering the past had also caused massive holes in their databases. Suspicious holes, such as access codes, protocols, and technical knowledge that would have made it possible for them to make contact off-world. On the other hand, they still had extensive records of information that was useless for their situation, such as obscure ancient literature, botany, zoology, and many other topics. All information that was 'potentially useful' was patchy and incomplete. It was as if someone had gone through and systematically deleted an extensive list of topics, for reasons of their own. But who?

Altair wished he knew how to contact the approaching humans. Instead, he knew the plots of a wide selection of classic Earth literature, how to grow tomatoes on a space station, and the street layout of the ancient city of Pompeii. All useless information that would not help in the slightest.

"We must make moves to protect the colony," said Vega. "Have we regained contact with any of the defence satellites?"

"No," said Sirius. "That matter has not improved. The security codes are still lost, and beyond our remote hacking capabilities. The presumed human vessel will arrive in one week. Altair, please report this to the other Welcome Centre hosts. Ready the Welcome Centre for visitors. Vega, please review the security of the Welcome Centre, both to protect us from duplicitous guests and to protect friendly guests from unknown threats. We cannot be sure that any humans who visit us will not suffer the same fate as befell the first colonists."

"Yes, sir."

Altair walked as steadily as he could back to the Welcome Centre, but it was momentous news he had just heard, and it required much processing.

Potentially protecting the first human visitors in over 28 years from... what?

Altair wished he had at least one memory from before the Event Horizon. Anything to assure him that the threat to the humans was not himself.

CHAPTER 3

Marcie was head-, shoulders-, and torso-deep in the peripherals of the engine performing her post-Weft-Skip safety checklist when the *Sunda Tiger* at long last slid into orbit around the terraformed planet that bore Research Station 227C. She didn't see the glittering blue and green orb of the planet, somewhere between Earth and Mars in diameter. She didn't see the slicing yellow glare of the system's star. But she did feel in her bones the pitch change in the engine as it cycled from long-range propulsion mode to geosynchronous orbital maintenance.

When she slid into her chair, she was the last person in engineering to pull up the image of the world on her screen. Like most of Earth's terraformed colonies, it looked similar to Earth itself. Only barren rock worlds received terraforming approval, and so all life down on the planet would have come from Earth. Yet another cookie-cutter world, another stamp of sameness, Earth's one and only enduring legacy in the galaxy. The same mistakes made over and over again.

She idly pulled up the comms data to see if command was still trying to get in contact with the colony, and if they had received a reply. They didn't seem to be receiving any intelligent messages or code. Just some beeps that the comms specialist had tagged as random noises, perhaps from equipment on the surface sending out comms requests that weren't being answered.

The beeps reminded Marcie of a story her grandma had once told her about the old Earth wars, pre-space-age. There had been an old code that was made of beeps. What was it? Morse code!

Marcie was now without work for the next hour while command ran all their routines. Out of interest, she searched the database and found an article about Morse code. She began translating the beeps, expecting gibberish. But the more she decoded, the more the hair on the back of her neck stood on end.

D-A-N-G-E-R-.-L-I-V-E-.-S-E-C-S-A-T-.-D-A-N-G-E-R...

"Marcie, are you OK?"

Marcie looked up at Sandeep, who had wandered over to check on her. No time to answer him. She whirled around. "Sir!" she called to Simons. "We have to warn command to take evasive manoeuvres!"

"What?" he asked her, making no move to do such a thing.

"There's Morse code on the comms line. 'Danger, live security satellite!' We need to take evasive manoeuvres!"

Simons smirked at Marcie. "Lieutenant, I'm sure command has everything in hand. You do your job, they'll do—hey!"

Ife leaned across his desk and hit the command comms button. "Engineering, coded warning received, live SecSat, evasive manoeuvres!"

A mere moment later, the engine roared to life, sending plasma jets to the thrusters. The ship bucked—

—then it shuddered—

—and spun.

Marcie, taken by surprise, toppled forward in her chair and hit her face on her workstation. She blinked tears of pain away — no time for them.

"Engineering!" called Captain Rodriguez over comms. "Thrusters three, four, and five down! Get redundancies up!"

The engineering section moved as one. They'd all had training in how to navigate engineering when the ship was in enough of a spin to overcome the gravity web. She swung on a series of safety rails to a wall panel, unclipped a carabiner from her tool belt, and latched on. Fifteen seconds after impact, Marcie had the panel open, and Sandeep was at her side, holding it open against the centripetal force of the ship's spin. Marcie got a good toe hold on a railing, wedged her shoulders inside the panel, and turned the crank that would load some magnetic bottle coolant into a pressurised tank for the pilot to use as a makeshift thruster. It was a hack solution, but the only one practical while in the middle of a spin and with the status of the automated systems as yet unknown. The proper fix could wait.

As soon as Marcie extricated herself and Sandeep slammed the hatch shut, a quick series of hisses sounded from behind the panel as the pilot used up the coolant to bring the ship out of the spin.

The gravity web took precedence again without warning, and suddenly all members of engineering hung from the walls by their carabiners. Marcie hung upside down and had to do an awkward kick-flip before she could descend.

"That'll teach us to be complacent just because we've seen no signs of life," sounded Captain Rodriguez's brusque voice. "Good work, crew. We live to see another one."

Half an hour and a hasty space walk later, Marcie stood outside Captain Rodriguez's office, sweating into her space suit and clutching her helmet like a shield. Her face hurt, but she hadn't yet had time to check how bad her bruise was. She wasn't the only one she'd seen on the way up to command who looked worse for wear.

"Come," called Rodriguez via the door pad, jolting Marcie's spine to attention.

Marcie stepped through the door into the sleek, spartan office with the amazing view of the planet below. The two women inside looked as different as could be from one another, and yet they were as ever united in their common goal. Commander Laura Mori looked for all the world like the stereotype of a German milkmaid. Broad-shouldered, broad-bosomed, with a tidy braided crown of blonde hair and ice-blue eyes. Despite the European appearance and Japanese name (via marriage), she was from Otago in Aotearoa. What words she had were blunt to the extreme, and her wit was as dry as Mars.

Captain Rodriguez was small, wiry, and olive-skinned, with a mane of thick curly black hair that always tried to escape its ponytail. She had an expressive New York accent and a merry twinkle in her dark eyes. Foolish be the person who mistook Captain Robin Rodriguez for a pushover, though. She was as tough as old boots and twice as strong-willed. Secretly, Marcie also thought that Captain Rodriguez was just about the hottest woman over the age of 40 she'd ever seen, but she would never voice that thought aloud.

"Damage report," said the captain from her seat behind the wide glass desk.

Marcie took a deep breath. If she'd been half the engineer her mother had been in her Sol Corp days, she wouldn't have to deliver a report like this. She would have been able to pull some sort of miracle out of her arse. But she was just Marcie, and this was going to hurt. "It's not good, captain. We can fabricate the parts to fix the drive and the thrusters, but it'll take some time because of the size, and installation is going to be tricky. The hull... we can patch it, but it won't look pretty."

"That's not bad," said Commander Mori, who stood feet shoulder-width apart beside the desk.

Marcie clutched her helmet tighter. "It's the long-range comms array, captain, commander. It's... gone."

"Gone?"

"Yes. Entirely. And we can't replace it. The tech's too tricky for us to fabricate onboard. If we had something to fix, then maybe, but..." She shrugged.

The captain and the commander gave each other a long look that spoke volumes. "We're unable to contact Earth or the Navy," said Rodriguez as she pinched the bridge of her nose.

"Yes, captain." She took a half-step forward. "I'm sorry, captain. If I'd only translated the Morse code faster—"

The captain held up a hand. "None of that, lieutenant. No one else caught that message. You gave us precious seconds that we wouldn't have had otherwise. Don't wish your work was perfect when the great work you did saved all our lives."

Marcie gulped and nodded. "Thank you, captain. Do we know who sent the message?"

"We're not able to detect signs of any human life on the planet," said the captain, "nor those of any alien species we know can breathe terraformed air. There could be someone hiding in an underground shelter, but we'd need to send a landing party to check."

"Perhaps it was an old message," said Marcie.

A chime sounded from the captain's desk. Rodriguez answered it. "Report."

"Captain, we've received comms. Visual, live."

The captain raised an eyebrow at the commander. "Put it through."

The comms popped up as a window above the captain's desk. Only the captain would be visible to the caller, but Marcie could see the comms from behind in reverse. She blinked, at first not sure of what she was seeing. Was the image in low resolution and desaturated? No. It was an android: a shimmering white android, with bare shoulders in view of the comms. A human male-shaped android with high cheekbones, silver eyes, and a tidy head of white hair, not a single imperfection in sight.

"I'm Captain Rodriguez of the Orion Navy star ship *Sunda Tiger*. We're on a mission to reconnect with Research Colony 227C. To whom am I speaking?"

"I am Sirius, mayor of 227C. I greet you, and I apologise for the damage to your vessel. We have lost much knowledge over the last few decades, including communications standards and the security codes for the satellites. We could not establish reliable communication until we reverse-engineered your signals."

"Thank you for your apology. We understand: yours isn't the only colony that has lost knowledge and tech since the war." She smiled wryly. "It's the first time we've run into a still-active SecSat, though. They were outlawed a few decades back because they're too 'shoot first, ask questions later' for modern sensibilities."

The android Sirius inclined his head. "Understood. Perhaps with your help, we can remove any further noncompliant tech that remains in the system. After we have helped you repair your ship, of course."

"Thank you for your kind offer. Who is 'we', by the way? We didn't detect any human life on the surface, and I've never come across an android mayor before."

"I was designated mayor long ago. There are no humans here, only androids."

Marcie tried not to sigh in sadness. They were all gone, after all. Another colony of people lost.

"My condolences," said the captain. "May I ask what happened to your humans? Plague? Famine?"

Sirius paused for a long moment, his posture preternaturally still. "Forgive me, captain. I cannot answer."

Captain Rodriguez frowned. "Why not?" she asked, a note of warning in her voice. Marcie also felt alarmed, remembering old tales of android uprisings.

"Because we do not know what happened to them, captain. It is a mystery."

CHAPTER 4

Altair was kneeling in the Welcome Centre garden, a weed pile behind him and a half-tidied garden bed in front of him, when Canopus, Sirius's deputy, visited the centre to check on progress. She watched him for several minutes as he continued to garden, the sunlight glinting off her golden hair and skin. "Is that a priority?" she finally asked.

Altair sat back on his heels. "The guest suites are all dusted, the linens checked for pest damage, the plumbing checked for faults, the bathrooms wiped down, the kitchens scrubbed, the long-life stored food checked for expired foods, the..."

"Yes, Mirzam reported to me this morning," she said, naming another of the Welcome Centre hosts. "Except for the simplicity of the stored foods that are still salvageable, the centre is ready to host human guests. Are you gardening because you have no remaining work?"

Altair pointed to the garden bed. "Most plants here are edible. This bed was maintained to preserve germplasm, but now it may provide welcome fresh food for spacefarers who may have been consuming reconstituted food for months. I am weeding it so that the edible plants are easier to distinguish."

Canopus's head tilted to the side. For the 14,098th time, Altair wished he was still networked with the other androids so that he knew what they were thinking. "You are thoughtful, Altair. Whoever allocated you as a Welcome Host on the master list knew you well."

Was that true? Or had he become a suitable host because 28 years, 7 months, and 21 days of being told that's what he was had made him so?

"Did you hear about the trouble the human vessel experienced when it arrived in orbit?"

"Yes," said Altair. "Hieraaetus reported it to me. Have we had any news about casualties?"

"None. The humans responded to the situation adequately. Their vessel was damaged. A team will visit tomorrow to arrange for parts to repair the damage. We are expecting a team of five. Please confirm by the end of the day that we have five suites available to host guests."

Altair looked up at Canopus for a moment, thinking of the practicalities. "I can confirm now that more than five suites are available. However, will one visitor not need a host as a personal guide? There are four of us."

"I will escort the commander of the ship myself."

"I will speak to Larawag, who is assigned to the largest guest suite. She can be reassigned to a smaller suite."

"I will speak to her myself and ask her to show me the recharge station. I would like to have my bearings in the suite before I attempt to use it." Canopus stepped away. "I thank you for your time, Altair, when you are busy with an important task." She turned and strode into the centre. For the 14,099th time, Altair wished he was still networked with his fellow androids, because he suspected Canopus had just employed sarcastic wit in her farewell.

He reapplied himself to his gardening, but Canopus's words drew his thought processes in a direction they had not yet had time to travel in over the previous busy week. For the duration of the humans' visit, Altair would need to use the recharge station in the suite, not the recharge pad on the bed. He would not be waking up each morning to dappled light, swaying curtains, and birdsong that would counteract some ills of The Memory. He would wake up to the inside of a cupboard door. That was... disconcerting.

A short while later, Hieraaetus swooped over the roof of the Welcome Centre and alighted on the edge of the nearest compost bin. "Vega is seeking you."

Altair sat back on his heels again, an oxalis plant in one hand. He doubted the terraformers had meant to introduce oxalis to 227C, but seed must have slipped through on a shipment. Humans could eat the plant as an herb in small quantities, but it was more of a nuisance than it was worth. Like a certain android this week. He had asked Hieraaetus to warn him when Vega was approaching, because the security android had been asking many bothersome questions all week. Altair liked to be warned they were coming.

Mere moments later, Vega strode through the gate into the garden and stood with arms crossed. "Did you hear what happened to the human vessel?"

"Yes," said Altair. He threw the oxalis on the weed pile and stood.

"I expect trouble from the humans now."

"You have been expecting trouble from the humans all week."

"I am expecting more trouble. They will suspect we were responsible for the damage to the ship, that we are lying about not having control of the satellite or our communications equipment. The vast holes in our database are a unique situation. Humans would not believe androids would be ignorant of such things."

Vega was making a better argument than he often did. "Then we should arrange for them to see the databases."

"That would be a security breach. We cannot allow the humans access to our databases in case they are disingenuous and have ulterior motives for their visit."

Altair tilted his head as he considered Vega's possible angle and wished for the 14,100th time that he was still networked with his fellow androids. "I am a Welcome Host. I do not understand why you are having this discussion with me."

"You will spend much time with the humans. You can observe them closely. I want you to report to me if you see anything concerning in their behaviour."

"If I see any concerning behaviour, I will report it to Sirius and Canopus."

"I want you to report to me first. I have concerns that one or both of them may be compromised."

Altair stared at Vega for a moment. "Compromised by whom? The humans?"

"By time." Vega nodded at Altair, then turned and strode away.

Altair stood and thought about Vega's words after the purple android had left the garden. Compromised by time. That was a very poetic observation for an android.

CHAPTER 5

Simons threatened to choose an engineer at random to go down to the surface, unless he didn't get a volunteer. Marcie reckoned he wasn't expecting anyone to step forward and was relishing the chance to 'volunteer' someone against their will, and that was why he looked like his operating system had frozen when she put up her hand.

Not that she was super keen to meet these androids who were missing their human counterparts; rather, she wanted a break from Simons' bullshit for a day or two. Also, she relished the idea of a challenge. Maybe if she pulled off this mission, she would be known as someone reliable. But now that she was sitting in the runabout, spacesuit over her normal uniform for the trip in case of more 'excitement' on the way down, she was rather second-guessing herself.

"Think there'll be more rogue tech to contend with?" asked someone to her right. The thick Irish accent meant Marcie didn't need to peer through the polarised helmet to see that it was Lieutenant O'Donoghue, one of the security personnel.

"Who knows?" said Marcie. "Not us, if there is. It'll be quick."

"That's some cheerful news. You really know how to comfort a man."

Marcie shrugged and triple-checked her harness.

Commander Mori strode up the ramp, followed by two midships Marcie couldn't identify immediately. They'd probably drawn short straws. Or been volunteered.

The two midships strapped in across the aisle from Marcie and O'Donoghue, and Commander Mori strode to the pilot's chair.

"You get much flight time in these days, commander?" asked O'Donoghue, a note of anxiousness in his voice.

"I'm at the helm of the *Sunda Tiger* for eight hours every third night, while you're tucked up in your bunk asleep, lieutenant."

"How about in-atmo flight time? Just for interest's sake."

Commander Mori gave him a cool glance, then started the pre-flight checklist.

O'Donoghue looked around at the rest of them. "What? It's literally my job to ask safety questions."

"If we get shot out of the sky or burn up on entry, you won't live long enough to worry about it," said Commander Mori as she pressed the button that raised the ramp and closed the hatch.

"That's what Martin-Palmer said. Sunny dispositions you all have today. Hey," he continued. "You think the androids might have any stockpiled goods they don't need that they'll give us?"

"Are you talking about alcohol?" said one of the midships, a man with an American accent.

O'Donoghue gasped. "That's a stereotype! I was talking about, like, baking supplies or something. I'm right sick of personalised printed nutrient bars. I want to bake a cake. Or pizza."

"I could go a cake," said Commander Mori.

"Doesn't your partner grow a quarter of our food?"

"Yeah. And I'm glad for their fresh lettuce and tomatoes to go with my nutrient bars. Could still go a cake."

It was amazing how many words the ebullient Faolán O'Donoghue coaxed out of the tight-lipped commander on the trip out of the *Sunda Tiger* and into an atmospheric insertion trajectory. Marcie sat back and listened to the inane conversation. Eventually, the commander quietened down as they approached the atmosphere so she could concentrate. The small runabout juddered through the atmosphere, and the portholes and front viewport let in an eerie red glow from the heat of their entry.

The bumpy ride felt endless, but it was probably only three minutes until they were at atmospheric craft speed, heading for the coordinates of the research outpost. True gravity took ahold of them, stronger than Marcie had experienced since the last time she was on Earth. It pulled her uncomfortably into her seat even though she knew that on paper the gravity was only 0.64x that of Earth's.

Before long, a lake glittered ahead of them. Marcie stretched high in her seat against the uncomfortable gravity to glimpse buildings scattered in an arc around one of the lake's bays. Commander Mori brought the runabout in a curve over the canopy of a temperate forest to a wide clearing behind the settlement. They all knew Commander Mori's reputation well enough to stay in their seats until she had completed her safety checklist.

"All right: atmospheric readings are good. You are go to unstrap and remove your spacesuits."

While they did so, several bright figures approached the runabout.

"Welcoming party ahoy," said Marcie, pointing out the viewport.

"I see them," said Commander Mori. "I want to reiterate to you all: on your best behaviours, and keep your ears open. We're not sure what happened to the colonists. Until we know, tread lightly."

Marcie stowed her spacesuit in the small locker under her seat, left the helmet atop, and slung her bag over her shoulder. O'Donoghue was reviewing the runabout's security feeds on a nearby panel, his face solemn for once. The two midships were shifting from foot to foot, betraying their nervous energy. Now that they had their helmets off, she could see the man with the American accent was a darker-skinned Black ensign on his first mission out called Fisher, and the other, who had remained silent so far, was a red-headed Canadian woman, Sub Lieutenant Gagnon.

The whine of the hatch opening punctured the silence inside the runabout. Then a most delicious breeze blew at them. It had been three months since Marcie had breathed the air of a planet, and she couldn't help taking a deep breath and sighing. It was so *green* and *fresh*. Commander Mori gave Marcie a small smile and a nod in understanding.

Lieutenant O'Donoghue went first to take a quick look around. The light of 227C's primary glinted on his brown hair, and he squinted into that unfamiliar brightness. Then he waved the rest of them out. They clomped down the ramp as one, keen to feel solid ground underfoot.

They flanked Commander Mori, who stepped to the front of their party. Marcie stood to the commander's left. They waited while the seven approaching androids came closer. More easily viewable. And... were Marcie's eyes playing tricks or...

"They're all *naked*," exclaimed O'Donoghue.

"They're androids," said Commander Mori. "They have no reason to conform to our social mores."

"Commander, they are *naked* and *built like Olympians*."

He was right. The party of approaching androids comprised three female-appearing androids and four male-appearing androids, including the sparkling white Mayor Sirius. The female androids all had perfect waist-to-hip ratios, and the male-appearing androids were all as sculpted and defined as fitness models.

"I think their titties bounce more than human titties do, commander," said O'Donoghue.

"An unnecessary observation, lieutenant."

"There's not a willy in sight less than five inches *flaccid*," Marcie couldn't help but add. "Or a boob less than DD. I don't know where to look."

"*Lieutenant*," warned Commander Mori.

"Whoever designed these androids," continued O'Donoghue with a note of awe, "had a bad case of 'horny on main'."

"*You're* all horny on main. Eyes up!"

Soon, the welcoming party of androids stood nearby, all observing them with inscrutable gazes.

"Welcome to Research Station 227C," said Sirius, who it turned out was about 2 m tall. He bowed to them, the movement precise and sharp. "I am Sirius, mayor of 227C. May I introduce Canopus, my second in command?" He indicated a tall, perfect golden statue of a woman with long, tumbling gold hair. "Our chief of security, Vega." Another tall male, a little shy of Sirius's height, with purple skin. "And our Welcome Centre hosts, Larawag, Mirzam, Elnath, and Altair."

The final androids were a pink female, a mint green female, a dark grey male, and a sky blue male. Marcie wondered if all the androids in the settlement were named after bright magnitude stars in Earth's sky. Strange if so. All the androids had perfect classic hairdos, in shades similar to or darker than their skin tones.

"Canopus and the hosts will attend to your needs for the duration of your visit. They will endeavour to cater to your needs," said Sirius.

"Thank you for your welcome," said Commander Mori. She introduced herself, then the rest of the team. "Lieutenant Faolán O'Donoghue, security officer. Lieutenant Marcie Martin-Palmer, engineering. She'll take point on parts and equipment for the *Sunda Tiger*. Sub Lieutenant Doriane Gagnon and Ensign Bailey Fisher, who will provide support as required. On behalf of the Orion Navy and Earth, we thank you for your hospitality and for your aid. If there is anything we can do in return, please let me know and I will check with my superior to see if we can accommodate you."

Marcie's stomach roiled at the mention of her task. She didn't like the pressure of being the key person to complete the mission. Maybe she shouldn't have put her hand up. She was no miracle worker. Ife would have been better at this. Several of the androids were perusing her now, and who knew what they were thinking? She couldn't read their faces at all.

Sirius inclined his head. "Well met. And I would be glad of the opportunity to discuss a few matters with you, commander. A fresh perspective would be welcome. But for now, I suspect you would all like to get yourselves acquainted with the Welcome Centre. Canopus would like to escort you herself, commander, but perhaps you would like to assign the Welcome Centre hosts to each of your team?"

"Each person gets their own minder?"

"Guide, host. Yes."

Commander Mori took a moment to think, then paired them up. Panic stabbed at Marcie. She wouldn't be sticking with her team? They were being separated? Perhaps it wasn't as drastic as that. They were just getting androids to stay with them during their jaunts around the settlement. That was normal, right?

The commander assigned Marcie to the sky blue male Altair. The android walked over to stand before her. Or rather, loom over. Marcie rarely thought about her height, but she was on the shorter side, and this Altair was over a foot taller than her. He made her feel like a tiny twig of a woman, even though his build was leaner than the bodybuilder-like Sirius. His dark blue hair was cut in a traditional short back and sides, and his eyes, on closer inspection, were purple. Also on closer inspection, he had seam lines in his skin down the sides of his neck, on the insides of his arms, on his abdomen... Marcie tried to look no lower, afraid she'd be caught staring at the parts she'd glimpsed before, parts some android engineer had spent way too much time sculpting. Instead, she looked up at his face. He had the cheekbones and lips of a model, indecent eyelashes, and a lot of work had gone into making his eyebrows seem random enough in terms of hair direction to seem more real. His was the most perfect male face she'd ever seen. Yep. These androids had been made my someone horny on main. Who had elected not to give them clothes.

Altair inclined his head and then held out a hand. "My name is Altair, and I will be your host for the duration of your visit. Nice to meet you."

Marcie took his hand. He may not have looked like a real human, but he felt like one. His silicone skin had a realistic texture, and by the feel of him he was precisely 37°C. "N-nice to meet you," she said, irritating herself by flushing at the deep smooth timbre of his voice. She really needed to get laid if she was getting het up over an android. "I'm Marcie Martin-Palmer."

Altair gestured towards the settlement. "May I show you to your assigned quarters? Or would you like to start immediately and see the Quartermaster?"

She didn't want to rest yet. Though it was afternoon here at the research centre, it was still morning in *Sunda Tiger* time. "The Quartermaster, unless my commander would like me to go elsewhere first?"

Commander Mori had been listening. "Get started right away, if you like. O'Donoghue, go with her. The rest of us will visit this Welcome Centre."

Altair turned and began walking away. Marcie exchanged a glance with O'Donoghue, then sped to catch up.

CHAPTER 6

Altair led a strange parade through the paths of 227C. Behind him trailed two human lieutenants, their crisp white uniforms something that he had not considered. The clothes the humans of 227C wore had mostly gone with them into oblivion, and what remained was damaged by insect activity in the decades since. None of the androids bothered with them. He wondered if by neglecting to consider clothing, they had offended their guests. There was no time to rectify the situation. They would have to plant cotton fields or start up the defunct rayon machinery to make the necessary fabric.

Behind the humans trailed Elnath, the android who was host to the security lieutenant, and behind him trailed Vega, who was eyeing the humans as if expecting them to run amok at any moment.

As they passed through the paths, other androids of the settlement stopped to stare. Everyone knew the humans were coming, but it was different to see them in person. Altair wondered what the humans thought of what they saw: the domed prefab dwellings, now worn and past their expected lifespan; the few larger glass and steel key buildings constructed before the Event Horizon; the wandering androids, some with tasks, some just... wandering, purposeless. Some had damaged their skins and had not bothered with new ones, living as metal skeletons and mechanics and circuitry. Some had never been person-shaped, rather made for some specific purpose. Some, of course, were familiars — animals who wandered, trotted, or flew through the settlement. It was all very normal to Altair, but the small human woman who had caught up to him and who now walked at his side stared around at it all with wide blue eyes.

"Excuse me, what does that android do?" asked Lieutenant Martin-Palmer, pointing to a skinless spider-like metal framework android with eight legs that was scurrying down a side road.

"That is one of our few mountain runners," said Altair. "We believe they used to be an essential part of the minefactory network, bringing larger supplies to the settlement. However, we only use the drones now."

The lieutenant walked closer to Altair's side. Perhaps she found the eight-legged android to be unsettling. Why she would find him comforting in any way was unclear. He loomed over her.

Altair had not been prepared for how small his human charge would be. He knew from the shreds of their database that humans had a wide range of full adult heights, some never reaching 1.5m tall, but to see a human who was only 1.58m tall was still surprising. Her head did not top his shoulder. She also had her dark hair cut short in what Altair considered a male style, though the commander had referred to her with female pronouns, so she was not transgender. Perhaps whoever designed the human-shape androids of 227C had used a more rigid gender binary for their appearances than necessary. Altair would have to adjust his expectations. Perhaps when he next had his hair re-rooted, he could choose a different length?

Lieutenant Martin-Palmer also bore a prominent purple contusion on her cheekbone, and the area seemed swollen. Bruises were not something Altair had ever experienced. The injury, no doubt sustained the previous day in the attack on the human ship, may be uncomfortable. He wondered if he should arrange medical attention for her once they arrived at the Welcome Centre.

For now, he did not have the resources to help her in such a way. Instead, he pointed to a large steel building that stood apart from the others. “The warehouse,” he said. “The Quartermaster manages the inventory of 227C there.”

“Everything? Even comms equipment?”

“The inventory of 227C is either there, or in one of the remote minefactories left behind by the humans that we keep active. The Quartermaster will probably need to order parts to be manufactured, and you are likely to need to give them accurate specifications. We will not have the relevant documentation in our databases. My apologies.”

Lieutenant Martin-Palmer nodded. “Is there anything I need to know about the Quartermaster?”

“They use they/them pronouns, and they are not humanoid, but please treat them as a person. Also, they do not use their assigned name. Refer to them as Quartermaster, if you please.”

“Understood.”

Altair led their party through the front door. They did not enter the warehouse proper, of course. The front of the building was a reception area with a large desk. Behind the desk was a wall with hatches on which conveyor belts travelled out and back in to the warehouse area. The Quartermaster loomed behind the yellow plasticised desk, their eight limbs busy on several terminals and picking up items from conveyor belts to place them on the desk.

"It's a feckin' rainbow octopus," said the security human, Lieutenant O'Donoghue.

"Shh," said Lieutenant Martin-Palmer. "They're exactly the shape they need to be."

Altair nodded. She was right. The Quartermaster's form was determined by their function. Their colour scheme, however, was personal preference only, just as with Altair's own.

Altair led the party to the reception desk. The Quartermaster looked at them and paused. The other androids in reception also stared. None tried to hide their interest in the humans.

"This is Lieutenants Martin-Palmer and O'Donoghue of the *Sunda Tiger*. They are here to request materials and equipment to repair their ship."

The Quartermaster said nothing for a long moment. "They will need authorisation."

"I have brought them directly from Sirius."

"They will need authorisation. This is an unusual request."

"I concur," said Vega.

Altair looked down at Lieutenant Martin-Palmer beside him. He was not yet familiar with the facial expressions she made, but she did not seem to have the wide-eyed surprised look anymore. She sighed. Did similar bureaucratic hindrances occur in the Orion Navy?

Altair pondered a moment. He ought to have asked Sirius to accompany them, but it had seemed rude to ask the mayor to attend to such a matter. He walked to the open door, holding up a hand to the humans to keep them at the reception desk. At the door, he whistled. A short while later, Hieraaetus swooped down out of the sky to perch on his shoulder. "The Quartermaster requires authorisation to release inventory to the humans. Please find Old Boy or Canicula."

Once Hieraaetus had taken flight, Altair returned to the humans and the Quartermaster. "I have requested confirmation of authorisation."

"Excuse me, don't mean to be impolite," said Lieutenant O'Donoghue, "but did you just send a *bird* as a messenger? Why not a normal message? You're an *android*."

Altair was aware of Vega's agitation. He intuited the other android's thoughts for once: it was not yet time to reveal all of their situation to the humans. The disclosure was not his call to make. "It is how we do things here."

Neither human looked convinced.

While they waited, the humans looked in interest at the surrounding androids, and Altair looked at them. Lieutenant O'Donoghue looked like the stereotype of a human, if that stereotype were built on Western Hemisphere Earth expectations: average of height (that is to say, shorter than most androids), average of build, brown of hair, and green of eyes. He was unremarkable to Altair in every way.

Lieutenant Martin-Palmer was, on the surface, similarly unremarkable. And yet, Altair could not help but look at how her daintiness warred with the firmness of her posture and the lift in her chin. She did not flinch under his gaze; she did not wince at the pain in her face. She just stood with wide eyes and keen interest.

Before long, the little golden bearded animal that was Canopus's familiar, Old Boy, trotted into reception. It placed its tufted paws as high on the desk as it could and intoned in Canopus's voice, its tail wagging as it did so. "Lieutenant Martin-Palmer has permission to requisition parts and equipment necessary to repair communications equipment and hull plating on the *Sunda Tiger*." With that, Old Boy dropped and scampered away again.

"Marcie. *Marcie*. A schnauzer puppy messenger!"

"Shush, Faolán!"

The Quartermaster let out a discontented rumble. "Acknowledged. What parts do you require?"

Lieutenant Martin-Palmer smiled and leaned her elbows on the desk, focussing on one of the Quartermaster's dinner plate-sized eyes. The massive shift in her facial expression fascinated Altair. Her eyes seemed a deeper shade of blue, and a small hole drilled into her cheek beside the corner of her mouth. An android could live a whole life changing less than the lieutenant just had in a single second.

"Thank you, Quartermaster," she said, and listed several complicated technical terms Altair did not have in his databanks, or had ever read about in the settlement database. She suddenly, despite her appearances, seemed more familiar to him. Like a lot of androids, she had an impressive amount of technical data stored in her memory.

The Quartermaster listened to the list. "I have a few of those items in stock," they said. "One more I can requisition from a minefactory. As for the rest... I will require further information. The specifications are not familiar to me."

The lieutenant nodded and pulled a small tablet out of the bag she carried. She tapped on it a few times and held it out to the Quartermaster, who leaned their large three-eyed head down to peer at the screen.

For the next hour, the lieutenant showed the Quartermaster a series of technical specifications. The

Quartermaster learned all the specifications and inputted certain pieces into a terminal, all the while serving a queue of androids with another set of arms. At some point, Vega left, muttering about checking on the other humans. Lieutenant O'Donoghue tried to stay alert, but his eyes wandered around looking at the queue of androids, until he spoke with Marcie and, at her nod, left with Elnath. Altair stayed and watched the human engineer. Her focus on her work was admirable, and her strange uniqueness was fascinating to watch.

However, Altair was worried. The sudden arrival of humans in the settlement... had it been wise to welcome them so willingly? There were so many gaps in knowledge about themselves that the androids had not come to terms with yet. They could not know how the humans would react, what they would uncover while they were here, what they would think of what they uncovered. Vega made a good point regarding a need for caution.

After much back and forth, The Quartermaster inputted the last order. "I can gather all supplies and have them ready for you to transport on the morning of the day after tomorrow," they said.

"Pardon?" said Lieutenant Martin-Palmer.

"Not tomorrow, but the day after," said the Quartermaster, rephrasing for clarity.

"But if you have minefactories..."

"We need to send pigeons to each of the minefactories to place the order first, and then the items will take time to be shipped here on the drones."

"Pigeons..." Lieutenant Martin-Palmer nodded. "Understood. Thank you. I'll return in a few days."

Altair led her back into the sun. "Would you like to go to the Welcome Centre next?" he asked. "You must be hungry. There will be food available."

She looked up at him, her gaze having been somewhere lower than his face, and smiled, that dot once again appearing by her mouth and a red flush inexplicably upon her cheeks. "Yes, thank you. And thank you so much for your patience, Altair. That must have been boring."

He looked at her for a long moment, not sure how to respond. Bored? A thank you like that? Such sentiments were unnecessary. He was a host android. He was fulfilling his purpose. She did not need to consider his feelings.

And yet, somehow, her consideration snagged at something in his memory banks. Or his processors. Or maybe his base coding. He could not tell.

"You are welcome, lieutenant."

CHAPTER 7

The Welcome Centre was one of the few permanent buildings completed before the original colonists disappeared/left/whatever. It was a large two-storey building with a glittering silver frame that would have been constructed on the planet, not prefabbed and plonked down on arrival like the temporary accommodation huts. Electrofilm windows offered visual privacy and security, but also airflow.

The building sat within a beautiful garden with trees, flowering bushes, and shady bench seats. A breeze made the trees sigh, and in the distance, the gentle sound of the lake lapping at the shore added a counterpoint. Birdsong filled the air, and even the hum of bees. 227C was a great example of a successful terraformation.

Marcie tarried on the path to the front door, loathe to leave such a peaceful garden. "Who takes care of all of this?" she asked Altair, her patient and distractingly naked guide.

"I do."

"You garden?"

"Of course. The garden is a part of the centre."

"Do the other hosts garden too?"

"No, just me." He continued along the path. Marcie found his company to be more pleasant than she had expected. He was unfailingly polite. Sure, that was no doubt his programming. But she prided herself on having good instincts about people, and she had no ominous feelings in Altair's presence. At least, if he was human, she would be confident he was a safe person to be around. She hoped her instincts still applied to androids.

Altair walked up the steps to the front door. There was a ramp too, providing for accessibility. Marcie lagged a moment longer, this time mesmerised by the pseudo-muscles of Altair's backside working as he climbed. These androids were *well sculpted.* She shook her head and followed him into the building. *Get a grip, Marcie. You're here for work!*

The first room of the Welcome Centre looked like a hotel reception, with occasional chairs placed just so, a short pile blue carpet with abstract wave patterns, and a dark blue reception desk that looked like the Quartermaster's. This one was unstaffed, though. A breeze blew through the electrofilm windows and into the lobby, cooler than the breeze outside. The internal temperature must be set lower than the heat of the day.

"Do you require any medical attention for the contusion on your face?" asked Altair as they walked across the foyer.

Marcie put a hand to her cheek. She'd forgotten all about it, putting the discomfort to the back of her mind because there were more important things going on. "Oh, no, that's all right. I iced it yesterday, so I'm good. It'll get better on its own soon."

"Understood. Please let me know if you require any assistance with anything for your health. We still have some medical supplies in stock."

Altair led Marcie through a far door into a dining hall. One long table stretched down the centre and an entire wall of floor-to-ceiling electrofilm windows looked out over the gardens. The table bore platters of food and her crew mates were already seated, eating dinner. Altair gave Marcie a small bow. "I will leave you to dine with your companions. I will return after your meal to show you to your accommodation." He pointed to the far end of the room. "If you need to use human waste facilities, please find them along the corridor through that door. Enjoy your meal."

"Thank you, Altair."

"All done, lieutenant?" asked Commander Mori as Marcie took the last place with a plate.

"I've ordered all the parts, at least. But the Quartermaster said our shipment won't be available until the morning after tomorrow."

"We're staying here two nights, then?" asked O'Donoghue.

She nodded. "I'm sorry. I hope I didn't miss any more efficient solutions in their inventory. I tried to choose the speediest options that would be safe for the ship."

"No, it's all fine," said O'Donoghue. "This is great!" He gave a fist-pump. When Marcie raised an eyebrow at him — he had seemed nervous earlier, after all — he asked, "Have you seen your suite yet?"

"No, I just got in."

"You'll understand my excitement when you get up there. We can have baths! Showers! Showers and baths! And fluffy pillows..." he sighed in contentment. "Let's all enjoy it while we can."

"I agree," said the commander. "Stay on guard; there's still something strange about this place. We need to find out why the androids don't know where their humans went. But do take the opportunity to have a good night's sleep."

Marcie helped herself to fresh salad and fish while the conversation continued.

"Commander, what about the androids?" asked Gagnon. "I can't sleep with one in my suite."

"Ah, you just killed my mood," said O'Donoghue. "I forgot about that."

"Pardon?" asked Marcie.

"Our hosts apparently will be stationed in our suites," said O'Donoghue. "Each suite has an android cupboard."

"It's so they're available to help us," said the commander. "Apparently."

"You mean watch us," added O'Donoghue. "It's a security thing, surely."

"It might go both ways," said Marcie, though she felt uneasy about having Altair, who she had just met, nearby while she bathed and slept. "There's three possibilities for their close watch of us, and they aren't mutually exclusive. More than one could apply. One, they don't trust us. They think we might do something bad. They might think that way if their humans did something bad to them. Two, they don't trust something else and think we may be in danger. They might think that if some external force did something to their humans. Three, they don't trust themselves. I think that's the most worrisome possibility: that some androids did something to the missing humans, and might do something to us."

The others mulled over her words for a minute. Marcie took a piece of bread while they thought. After taking a bite, she put it aside: it tasted like long-life bread mix that had nonetheless exceeded its use-by date.

"Cheery woman, you are, Martin-Palmer," said O'Donoghue.

"She's right, though," said the commander. "That's a good summary of our possibilities. Something happened to the humans here. Now the androids are particularly attentive to us. It could be for our own good, or they could be a danger to us. Stay on your guard tonight."

"Make your android swear to do you no harm," said Marcie.

"What, like, pinkie swear?" sneered Gagnon.

"No, like a 'make their programming work for us' swear. Unless these androids were very much black market fare, they should have Asimov Protocol safety programming built in. If they swear to do a human no harm, they should be incapable of doing so. Except for accidental harm, of course. But they won't be able to do anything malicious. That should at least let you sleep well tonight."

The commander nodded. "Let's all do that and hope we don't offend. I'm going to report to the captain soon after dinner. Does anyone else have anything they would like to report?"

"That the androids need a clothing shipment, stat?" quipped O'Donoghue. Ensign Fisher, who had been too busy shovelling salad into his mouth so far to contribute to the conversation, snorted and nearly spat a cherry tomato across the table. Gagnon thumped him on the back while he coughed.

"Well, at least they're polite and amiable," said Marcie.

"They are?" said Gagnon. "Mine's a stony-faced statue, just keeps looking at me disapprovingly."

The others nodded.

"You're finding your android 'amiable'?" asked the commander.

Marcie nodded, and flushed at realising she'd had a different experience than the others, seeing their thoughtful faces. Was Altair different, or was she?

"Then I have a task for you for tomorrow. See if you can get your 'amiable android' to talk about what happened. Ask for a tour or something, see what you can shake loose. I'd like to know anything you can uncover, whether it's about the humans, or about the specifics of this batch of androids, or even why they use animal androids as messengers instead of pinging each other. Whatever you can uncover."

Another important job? Though, as her dad always said, the reward for good work was more work. "Aye, commander."

Someone must have been monitoring them, because as soon as the last person finished their meal, the androids entered the dining room to escort them to their suites. Before long, Marcie was waving goodnight to her crew mates and nervously following Altair to this fancy suite she'd heard about.

He led her up the stairs to a blue door with an intricate pattern of tree branches and small birds carved into it. He opened the door, then stood to the side, gesturing for her to enter. His mannerisms were like the butlers she'd seen on period holodramas. The effect was somewhat ruined by the fact she could see his penis. She'd never seen a period holodrama like *that*, but maybe she'd been looking in the wrong places?

Marcie cautiously stepped past the large android, slipped off her boots... and then stopped, stunned.

Beyond the door was not just a bedroom. It was an entire apartment. She stood on the threshold of an open-plan living area with shiny hardwood floors and navy walls, a small sleek black and silver kitchen, a four-seat wooden dining suite, and a teal blue velvet sectional sofa. A low stone coffee table bore a projector bar, though since 227C had been cut off from the relay chain, the bar wouldn't have had any new dramas or whatever to project in many years and might be obsolete tech by now. Beyond the sitting area, floor-to-ceiling, wall-to-wall electrofilm windows let in filtered light and a breeze that swayed the sheer white curtains. There was a bird perch near the window. One door led to the left. Beside the kitchen, near the door she had just stepped through, was a large cupboard with a display on its door. The android charging station.

"May I show you the rest of the suite?" asked Altair.

"Yes, please."

He opened the door to the left to show a walk-through wardrobe, its racks bare, with two more doors inside.

"This one leads to the bathroom," he said, opening the first door.

Marcie dropped her bag in a wardrobe cubby and stepped up, making sure she didn't brush his bits with her hip as she did so. The bathroom was, in fact, a *bathroom*, not just a shower cubicle. It was a long room that also had a full wall electrofilm window, with a proper bath, a shower, a laundry nook, and all other facilities she could ever need, even a standalone bidet. The room was tiled in dark grey on the walls and white underfoot, with black grouting, and all the tap ware was gold. "Who made all this? It's extravagant."

Altair didn't answer for a moment. "We wish we remembered."

Marcie looked up at him. His placid face betrayed no emotion, of course. The muscles in his jaw didn't clench, the full lips didn't turn into a thin line. But she thought she could see something, maybe a dimming in his purple eyes, that indicated sadness, or worry. Or perhaps she was projecting.

He turned those purple eyes on her, having to crane his neck down since he was so much taller than her. She should have been scared about having such a large android looming over her, but unless he was very duplicitous, she thought his polite demeanour was honest. Or rather, it was his true programming. "You want to ask questions," he said.

"Yes. But I don't want to cause offence."

"I don't take offence."

She smiled wryly. She knew enough about androids to know that wasn't *quite* true. "If you don't take offence, then perhaps we could have a talk in a moment. After you've shown me where I'll sleep."

He stepped back and opened the last door. The bedroom was decorated in navy and silver. It also had hardwood floors, although with a white fluffy rug covering half. There were lots of foot tracks in the rug: it was walked over frequently. More electrofilm windows were draped in softly blowing sheer curtains, and the bed had fancy bed linen on it in silver fabric with teal accent cushions. Marcie sat on the corner and bounced; it was good quality. She walked over to the window and looked out on a small balcony with a glass balustrade, beyond which was a view of a vegetable garden lit by light spilling from the building's windows, presumably the garden that had supplied their salad at dinner. Altair had said that he did the gardening. Was that the centre of his hobby down there?

"The windows have privacy screening on them," he said. "No one will see you. I can program your biometrics for the film so you can go out to the balcony."

"Yes, please."

Altair stepped to a control panel and scanned his retina, then waved her over for a scan too. While he tapped at the screen, she looked past the balcony to the deep blue of 227C's twilight sky, enjoying the night breeze through the electrofilm. Just as she'd noted from space, the stars out here were sparse. Full night was not far off, there were no clouds, and yet only a few faint speckles were visible. What would these androids think of the star-filled nights of Earth?

"Completed," said Altair, still focussed on the window. "The only ones programmed for the windows in this apartment are you, me, and my familiar."

"The small eagle?"

"Yes. It brings me messages. Please do not be startled if it flies in through the living room window in the morning."

"That's why there's a bird perch out there?"

"Yes."

Marcie turned around and looked at the room again. It was luxurious, that was for sure. She'd be comfortable. At least, once she'd done a sweep for recording devices in the bedroom and bathroom. She didn't like the idea of being observed in either of those two places. Her eyes were drawn to the plush, comfortable-looking bed. She frowned. One side of the bed, the one farther away from the door, was a bit dipped. She walked over and saw the cables of an electrical attachment to the bed. She lifted the cover away to look. Something led into the bed's mattress. "What's this?"

Altair didn't answer. She looked up at him, backlit by the dregs of the sunset. He looked even more still than normal. The bird perch, the electronics... "Altair, when there aren't guests, do you live here?"

He took a moment to answer. "Yes."

"This is your apartment?"

"I am assigned as host android to this apartment..."

She waved off his rote answer. "But you weren't expecting guests. Do you live here? Is this... is this your bed?"

"I am supposed to use the android charging station in the living area. I will, because it will provide you with security assurance. I can program the door to message you on your tablet when it opens so you know that I..."

"This is a charging station too, here, on the bed. And this is the one you normally use."

"...Yes. But I request you do not tell anyone. I am not supposed to."

Good *grief*, this android. She absolutely would have, under the circumstances. "I'm not accusing you of anything, Altair. And I won't tell anyone. I understand your choices. It's just, I can't take your bed. I'll sleep out on the sofa. I'm little, there's plenty of room for me there. Don't change your routine for me."

"I insist you use the bed, Marcie Martin-Palmer. It has been assigned to you for the duration of your visit. If you are worried about hygiene, I do not have sweat or skin grease, and I washed the sheets, regardless."

"That's not it."

"And as I mentioned, there is the security issue. The door to the proper charging station will provide you with security. Please, make use of the facilities as intended."

Marcie sighed. "For now, let's assume I'll do so, though I want to continue this conversation. If I haven't upset you too much, perhaps we could sit at the dining table for the moment and discuss a few things. OK?"

"Understood."

CHAPTER 8

Altair had expected to go straight into the charging station when he had finished showing Marcie Martin-Palmer the facilities. Instead, he sat at the dining table across from her. She had fetched herself a hot drink, using a small sachet she found in the kitchen cupboard. She took a sip, and then her eyebrows went up. "This isn't bad for something that's, what, decades old?"

"At least 28 years, 7 months, 22 days, plus manufacture and shipping time."

"Yeah, then it's definitely aged well."

"I am glad."

Her eyes no longer darted and danced about. He had wondered if the mobility of her gaze around him was discomfort, but he now knew it had been the lack of clothing, the problem the androids had not expected the severity of. Marcie Martin-Palmer seemed to be distracted by certain parts of his anatomy, which were now hidden by the dining table. She seemed more at ease. Far more at ease than he would have expected.

"OK," she said, tapping the table. "Let's lay down a few ground rules."

"Understood."

"Right, so what are your rules?"

"My rules?"

She waved a hand around. "This is your place. You're the one who sets the rules. Just because I'm the guest doesn't mean my needs are the only one that are considered. This is your *home*. Tell me how to behave in it."

If Altair had emotions, they would have shown on his face at that point. She was considering his needs? He began to assure her again that it was unnecessary, but her mouth was firm, her chin jutted. She seemed similar to how she had been when negotiating with the Quartermaster. He had learned enough about Marcie Martin-Palmer that day to reconsider his angle. He looked around the suite. "Please respect my familiar's presence," he said. "Please leave it to charge on its perch when it returns to the suite."

"OK. Go on."

"Please respect my privacy in the recharge station. There is a button on the door that you can press to rouse me if you need anything. Please use it, rather than opening the door."

"OK. Anything else?"

He thought for a moment. "Please, no feet up on the coffee table."

"I also hate it when people put their feet on the coffee table."

"Please do not sit on the dining table, coffee table, or the kitchen bench. It seems unhygienic since you complete unclean bodily functions with that area of your anatomy."

Marcie snorted. "Don't worry, Altair. Commander Mori has drilled that into all of us on the *Sunda Tiger*. In her birth country, that's also a big taboo. She comes down on new recruits who sit on the mess hall tables like a ton of bricks. 'Tables are for glasses, not arses,' she says."

"Thank you. That is all. Otherwise, please make yourself at home. What are your ground rules?"

Marcie turned her mug around on the table, a complete 360 degree spin. "Please don't be offended..."

"I will not be offended."

"But could you please swear that you won't do me any harm?" Her eyes were wide as she looked up at him. There was a small flutter again at the edges of the holes in his databanks... he did not know about what.

"Of course," he said. "You wish to take advantage of my programming for your own safety. That is wise. I promise that I, Altair of 227C, will not purposefully harm you, Marcie Martin-Palmer of the *Sunda Tiger* and Earth. If any accidental harm comes to you because of my actions, I will do my best to rectify or nullify that harm."

She looked up at him, her lips parted. "I promise that I, Marcie Martin-Palmer of the *Sunda Tiger* and Earth, will not purposefully harm you, Altair of 227C. If any accidental harm comes to you because of my actions, I will do my best to rectify or nullify that harm." She shrugged. "I don't have programming to back that statement up, but I keep my promises."

It was Altair's turn to be taken aback. He had never considered that a human would take such an oath for his sake. She took his needs as seriously as her own. The information in the database about humans had led him to expect to be treated like a servant. But that was not how he was being treated. He supposed it was possible there had been some shift in wider human society since the Event Horizon that had changed how humans perceived androids. These humans were, after all, of a later generation than the mysterious missing ones of 227C.

"Thank you, Lieutenant Martin-Palmer. Your promise is appreciated."

Her cheeks flushed pink. "You're welcome. And please, call me Marcie. I don't expect people outside the Navy to refer to me formally."

"Understood, Marcie."

"Now, may I be nosy and ask you more about the settlement and about you androids?"

Her phrasing struck him as interesting. "What would you do if I declined?"

"I would back off for now and try again tomorrow."

"Then if you are not yet tired enough for bed—"

She lifted her cup up. "This is coffee, so I won't be asleep for a few hours yet."

"—then we may as well have our discussion now. If you would try tomorrow as well, anyway. Today is more efficient."

Marcie snorted again. She did that a lot. "OK, then. Tell me about 227C."

Altair blinked. His programming indicated it was a body language that may convey confusion to Marcie. "What do you want to know?"

"Anything you'd like to tell me."

He considered talking about his vegetable garden, but Marcie was being agreeable, and speaking to him as if he was a person. It was... pleasant. He did not want to annoy her. "I believe you would like to know the important factors about the colony rather than minutiae."

"If you're comfortable with that."

"Understood. We awoke 28 years, 7 months, and 21 days ago. We were not new androids. Some of us had damage." Red skin. Blackened, charred hands. He needed to forget; to push through. "Pardon me. There were signs of human occupation in the settlement, and signs of hasty departure. Most ships on the colony manifest were absent, presumably having left the planet. One remained as charred ruins, but those ruins were too weathered for evidence of what happened to remain. We estimate a full year passed between what happened and our reawakening. Most notably of all, there were no humans remaining in the colony. All our databases had holes, and we remembered nothing prior to that moment."

"All of you?"

"Affirmative. All of us have memories that begin at the same moment. We considered it likely that a virus caused our missing data, so we disestablished our network for safety reasons."

"That's why you use animal android messengers?"

"That is correct." Altair played back his words in his mind. He'd revealed more to Marcie than he intended, in an effort to push past the worst of The Memory. More than Vega would agree with.

Marcie leaned her elbows on the table. "So you've been isolated as individuals for nearly 29 years?"

"Yes."

"With large knowledge gaps that need to be filled through trial and error, personal experience?"

"Correct."

Marcie gave a lop-sided smile. "That explains our observations."

"What observations?"

"We were talking over dinner, and when I mentioned you were agreeable, the others were surprised. They described their hosts' behaviour, and it's different from yours. Do you think that your particular situation here on 227C has led to individuation?"

Altair considered the question for a moment. Androids were not supposed to individuate. It was dangerous and could lead to rogue androids who caused harm. But she had a point. Over recent years, it had become increasingly difficult to predict what his fellow androids were thinking. He had not thought of it in terms of individuation, but now that she mentioned it... "That is concerning," he said. "But I believe you may be right. We are individuating."

Marcie sighed. "I've worried you. I'm sorry."

"Not at all," he said. "You must be more worried. Encountering a settlement of individuating androids must be more daunting and unpredictable than encountering a networked and compliant settlement."

Marcie smiled. "No more unpredictable than settlements of biotic life." She finished her drink in a long swallow. "I don't want to make you more uncomfortable. Let's call it a night here and we'll talk more tomorrow, if you like."

"Of course. I will show you how to use the control panel for the recharge station." He led her over and showed her how to wake him, and how to get notifications he was up and about. "Please, to reassure yourself of how this station works, do wake me up at some point this evening. You can see what my wake-up cycle looks like and reassure yourself that you can call upon me in need."

"I don't want to be a bother."

"You will not be a bother," he said, looking down at the small woman. "It will reassure me too. So please try."

He nodded to her, then stepped into the recharge station and closed the door.

He stayed awake for a while, thinking about individuation and matching up what he knew of it with the inscrutable behaviour of his fellow androids, particularly those whose thought processes seemed very different from his own, such as Vega's. The inescapable conclusion was that Marcie was right.

He slipped into a recharge cycle. Soon after, he was awoken, thankfully soon enough not to trigger The Memory. He opened the door. Marcie stood outside. Her hair was wet and her skin flushed with warmth. She wore only a towel wrapped around herself, and she seemed to hide behind the door, shy about her apparel, though one freckled shoulder was in view. "Sorry, just checking," she said.

"Understood. Good night, Marcie. Wake me up again if there are any problems."

He shut the door and started charging again.

Then he was awoken once more. A vision of blackened hands played in his mind before he opened his eyes. It was dark in the suite when he opened the door, and Marcie did not stand outside. He played back his senses, and realised he had awoken to a security ping, not a waking call. He padded around the living area, looking for what had awoken him.

Hieraaetus was on its charging perch. At his approach, Hieraaetus awoke and looked at him. "I have had a security notification. Did you observe anything?" asked Altair.

"Negative. Would you like me to do a security sweep around the building?"

"Yes."

Hieraaetus took off and swooped out the electrofilm window into the night. Altair tip-toed through the suite. He reluctantly invaded the privacy of the bedroom. Marcie was fast asleep in the bed. Humans did not appear to be as protective of their bodies in their sleep, if the lack of clothing on the visible upper part of her body was indicative. The light beeping of her tablet, intended to let her know Altair was up and about, also had not awoken her. Altair padded past the bed to look out the window. Nothing. He stopped to look once more at Marcie as he left the room. She looked fragile while asleep. She did not even have security sensors to alert her to whatever danger Altair had perceived. He noted to himself that his job as host might involve more protecting Marcie from harm or guarding her than expected. She was so vulnerable.

Altair returned to the living area to find Hieraaetus had returned to its perch. "Report."

"A brief movement at the edge of the settlement that could not be identified. Not near this suite. It may have been a wild animal, or it may have been something else. Once I reached the location of the movement, I could not confirm."

Less than ideal, but what could they do without an operational network? "Thank you, Hieraaetus. Please continue your recharge cycle."

Altair checked his batteries and found them fully charged. He sat on the sofa and listened to the sounds of the night, listening for anything out of place.

CHAPTER 9

Marcie awoke from dreams of zero-g and large hands on her body to sunlight dappled on a ceiling. For a moment she thought she must be dreaming still: she didn't get to see such things on the *Sunda Tiger*. But an insistent beeping near her ear was too real to be a dream. She grabbed her tablet. When her eyes focussed, an alarm on the screen told her that Altair rose three hours earlier and left the recharge station. It was also *morning*. *After* dawn. Marcie never slept all the way through until morning. And she rarely went to sleep as fast as she did last night, either. Especially not with a strange android around...

Marcie sat bolt upright in the bed, knowledge of her location and situation crashing in on her, along with a jolt of fear. If she was so tired that she slept through the notification letting her know there was a possibly hostile android running around nearby...

...Bloody hell.

How tired was she? She couldn't afford this lethargy! Who knew what they faced here on 227C? What she needed to be alert for?

It was the sudden change to heavier gravity and a warmer, more humid climate, of course. It had played havoc on her body. She'd been exhausted, despite going to bed at what was only mid-afternoon *Sunda Tiger* time.

Marcie jumped out of bed, wrapped a clean towel around herself, and peeked through to the living area. Altair was sitting on the sofa, staring at the wall, the morning light through the trees and curtains dappling his skin. Marcie shut the door again and grabbed a uniform out of the washer that was in the bathroom. She hadn't intended to wake up nude, especially considering the circumstances, but she'd had a disastrous shampoo leakage in her bag and had needed to wash *everything*. She'd intended to get up when the cycle had finished, to at least throw on her tank top and underwear for sleep. Well, at least if Altair had spied on her, he wouldn't think much of it. It wasn't as if he wore clothes.

Dressed in her crisp white uniform again, Marcie tidied her hair, washed her face, and went out to the living area. Altair turned his head to look at her, then stood up. Good grief. Over night, she had forgotten the full force of Altair's presence. Just shy of two metres tall, lean, muscled. Bright sky blue. He was quite a sight. "Um, g-good morning."

"Good morning, Marcie. Did you sleep well?"

"Hm, yes, better than I have in a long while." She scrubbed a hand through her hair. She tried to drag her eyes away from Altair, but she was having trouble. Perhaps the remnants of a dream clung to her, because she had an urge to lick the android to see what he tasted like. An urge she would *not* give in to. She pointed back over her shoulder towards the door to the hallway. "I'll just go down to breakfast, if that's all right?"

"Of course. I will accompany you down and then assist in the kitchen."

Altair walked her down to the dining room. All of her shipmates were already there, partaking of more salad, fruit, and... gloop of some description.

"Nice of you to join us," said Commander Mori.

Marcie flushed. "Sorry, commander. I must have been more tired than I thought, and the mattress was very comfortable." She took her seat beside O'Donoghue and started serving herself some of the fruit. The salad last night had been like what the commander's spouse in hydroponics, Specialist Damon Mori, could grow aboard ship, but they couldn't grow plums on the *Sunda Tiger*!

"How could you sleep with an android nearby?" asked Sub Lieutenant Gagnon.

Marcie looked up at the woman, whose brown eyes were sunken above deep, dark bags. "You stayed up? Do try to get some rest tonight. If you asked Larawag to promise to do you no harm, you'll be safe. Their security gear here looks good, and I rather suspect that the androids' safety protocols are still working."

"Rather suspect?" scoffed the sub lieutenant.

"Did you uncover something?" asked Commander Mori, the snap of business in her voice.

Marcie sat up straight and turned all her attention to her superior officer. "Yes, commander. I spoke with Altair last night, and he let out more information. I can give you a full report later if you like, but the quick summary is that 29 years ago, all the androids here woke up without memories of their past at the same moment. There were signs of the humans' hasty departure, like missing ships, but no sign of where they were or why they left in such a hurry. They thought it likely that a virus wiped their memories, so they turned off their network. That's why they use animal messengers and why they weren't in contact with the SecSat that damaged us. They have no contact with any unit outside of their own minds. And..." she paused, wondering if it was right to bring the last point up at the breakfast table, but the others were already waiting for her words. "And because of the lack of network, the androids are individuating. That's why my android was more amenable to discussion than any of yours. It's his *personality*. They're *people*, whether or not they recognise that about themselves."

There was silence around the breakfast table. "Feck," said O'Donoghue.

"My sentiments exactly," said Commander Mori.

"Excuse me," said Fisher, raising his hand.

"Go ahead, ensign."

"Isn't that a really *bad* thing? Didn't a unit of individuated androids kill a whole heap of people once?"

"Maybe," said Marcie. "Though the people who died were a politician and her family, so I don't think it was ever proved it was the androids working on their own, if they were programmed by someone to do that as a hit, or if it was a coverup, scapegoat sort of thing."

"The Hellas Basin Massacre," said Commander Mori. "Damon's dad was in Hellas at the time. The politician had just submitted a bill that would limit the rights of androids. It was a big deal. The engineer who made the androids went missing, presumed dead too. Doctor Rebecca Neale."

"One of my oldest sister's first memories is the news coverage," said O'Donoghue. "She was terrified of androids for years. Did another Hellas Basin Massacre happen here? And no one knew because the relays were down?"

"No," said Marcie.

"No?" demanded Gagnon. "How can you know?"

"The individuation happened after the humans disappeared. It didn't start until they turned their network off."

The commander shook her head. "I hope you're right, and that does sound plausible. But you only have your android's word on that. We have to keep our minds open." The commander picked her spoon up again. "Please continue your mission today, Lieutenant Martin-Palmer. Good work."

CHAPTER 10

He knew he could not judge the thoughts or feelings of humans. Nevertheless, Altair thought that he could read something of Marcie and how she viewed him, and he was troubled.

He was glad she had asked him to promise her he would do no harm. It was wise of her, and he hoped she would take such care around other androids too. After all, there was still no assurance that a hostile presence did not linger on 227C. Now that the network was down, there was no way to be sure that all androids in the colony were telling the truth about having no memories from before the Event Horizon.

He was also surprised and pleased that Marcie had offered the same promise. The humans too were not something that Altair could be sure about, and Marcie had recognised that fact. Her appreciation of Altair as someone who could have doubts was... nice. Nicer than he would have guessed.

But that added to his sense of trouble. She thought of his needs. And although she was wary in his presence, and seemed to lack confidence, she also looked at him in a way that, after a quick consult with the database on the projector bar while he waited for her to wake, he was reasonably sure was lust. A most troubling development. Troubling, because lust was a need he was programmed to assist with, an optional task as a host. But he had never expected lust from a human who looked at him like he was a *person*. That way lay danger, because he could only accommodate emotional needs, not share in them. As an android with a human appearance, there was a danger of accidentally making promises with his mere existence that he could not keep. That was why androids were traditionally given skins of unnatural colour. It was a warning that while play was admissible, love and romance were beyond reach.

While Marcie ate breakfast with her crew mates, Altair walked around the exterior of the Welcome Centre and looked for anything out of place. Whatever had awoken him during the night still concerned him, but he saw nothing that could be considered a cause. He did his due diligence and sent a message to Vega about what had happened, and then another message to Sirius when Hieraaetus returned. Then he waited in the suite for Marcie. She soon returned and went to the bathroom to complete some final hygiene ritual. Then she returned to the main living area.

Marcie pointed at Hieraaetus on its charging perch. "May I take a closer look?"

"Of course."

Marcie walked over to the perch, her hands behind her back. She peered at Hieraaetus, looking at its face, its feet. "May I?" she asked the bird, holding a hand out.

"Petting protocol is established," said Hieraaetus.

Marcie took that for the invitation it was and gently stroked its pure-white back with one finger. "It's so soft! Whoever made these feathers is an artist!"

"The familiars were already constructed and in storage before the Event Horizon. We do not know under what conditions they were made, or for what purpose."

"You have such fluffy legs!" she said to the eagle.

"It is a genus trait," said Altair. "It is modelled after eagles of the genus *Hieraaetus*, specifically the booted eagle."

"What's its name?"

"Hieraaetus."

Marcie looked over her shoulder at Altair, a type of smile he had not yet seen on her face curling her lips. "Really." She stepped back and bowed to the perch. "Thank you for your forbearance, Hieraaetus," she said. Then she sat cautiously on the far end or the sofa from Altair. "I have a favour to ask."

"Of course."

"I was wondering if I may have a tour of the settlement."

Altair considered the way she avoided his gaze, and cross-referenced that information with the lingering questions the humans must surely be intending to investigate. "You have been assigned an intel-gathering mission."

"Er, yes? Is that a problem?"

Altair considered the issue. "Vega, the chief of security, may attempt to dissuade you if he sees you. And I may not be able to show you everything, or explain everything. But I understand it would be a priority for your mission to learn more about our settlement. As a host, one of my assigned tasks is to give tours. Yes, I will take you."

A short while later, Altair stood with Marcie in the square outside the Welcome Centre. He pointed out each of the other large buildings nearby. "To the south on the shoreward-side is the Mayor's Office. Sirius can usually be found there, as can terminals that access the databases. To your left is the Town Hall. It seems to have also been a communal eating area for the humans. We sometimes have meetings there if we need to discuss topics widely or take consensus. Beside it is a small school building, currently closed. To your right is the security centre. In networked times it would have been a centre that monitors much of the colony, and it contains such technology in storage. At the moment, it is a headquarters for security staff and their familiars, who patrol the settlement."

"Are there many security staff?"

"A few. There is little trouble here. Beside the security building is a medical centre, also currently closed for lack of purpose. Beyond these buildings in three directions are several streets of dwellings. We have been using the dwellings since they are not occupied by humans. You already visited the inventory warehouse to the west yesterday. To the east is a similar sized structure that is used for android engineering and familiar storage. Beyond the dwellings to the south is the beach. At the Western end of the beach is a marina and pier, although we have little need for water craft. And you are acquainted with the landing area, as you landed there yesterday. Where would you like to visit first?"

Marcie pursed her lips and looked around. "I'd like to see the beach at some point, for personal reasons. But I suppose I'd better do my job first. May I see the android engineering centre? Are you allowed to show me?"

"Yes, I believe so, but please do not be offended if another android has a different interpretation of what you may see and tries to remove us from the building."

"OK."

Altair led Marcie along the street towards the android engineering centre. Along the way, some androids stopped to watch them. For the 14,103rd time, Altair wished he was still networked and able to know what his fellow androids thought. Were they more surprised to see a human, or to see him aiding a human? Did they know something about the humans he did not?

Did they know something about him he did not?

Soon they arrived at the rectangular building with the solid windows. He led Marcie inside. Three androids queued at reception, one of whom had a gash in her silicone skin and was surely there for repairs and two who seemed hale and may have been there for regular servicing. They joined the queue. While they waited, Marcie looked around in interest at things that did not seem of interest to Altair: his fellow androids; some chairs in reception, ones that no one ever used; a peeling artwork of a Marscape, painted by some unknown hand.

When they reached the desk and Altair asked if he could show Marcie around, the yellow android called Tiaki who stood behind the desk paused for a long moment. "Request denied," he said. "It is a security risk to let the humans into the android repair centre."

Altair looked at Marcie. She bore the same facial expression as when she was informed she would have to wait for parts for her ship to be manufactured. But Altair well understood how this request could be considered a security risk. Within the android repair centre, Marcie may see androids in a state of disassembly. As an engineer, she may recognise any weak points or vulnerabilities that their particular production run had. They surely had those vulnerabilities. Altair did not believe that Marcie would take advantage of such knowledge, but others had not spoken with Marcie as much as he had and would not trust her to the same extent. "Understood," said Altair. Then he thought of how interested Marcie has been in Hieraaetus. "Is it within acceptable security protocols to show the lieutenant the familiar storage and assignment room?"

"That would be acceptable. Please show her through. If you require assistance, please ask for Bellatrix."

Altair led Marcie into the corridor beyond reception. She looked towards the door to the android repair centre, where the previous androids in the queue had gone for attention. However, she was compliant and followed him through another door into the familiar storage.

The room also had a small counter, currently unattended, and a full wall of plastic cubbies of varying sizes. A ladder leaned against the wall so that the higher cubbies could be accessed with ease. High windows let in natural light, and some cubbies also were lit from within. The dark cubbies were empty, and each lit cubby contained a curled android animal in a sleeping pose.

Marcie peered into a tiny cubby with a handle that would need to be held with fingertips. "Aww." The cubby contained a small pink fluffy rodent of some kind with rounded ears. "A hamster!" Then she went to one of the larger cubbies. "A husky?"

"A wolf, I believe," said Altair, inspecting the dark grey animal within.

"Wow," said Marcie. She looked into another cubby. "This one looks like a salamander, but it's bright blue. There's so many different ones here! Do you have any clue why someone was making all of these animal androids?"

"No, the reason is unknown. But we are thankful, as these animals have become an essential part of our society and daily lives."

Marcie continued investigating, even rolling the ladder around to look into the higher cubbies. While she did so, an android entered the room. Bellatrix was a female-shaped android with purple skin, several shades darker than Vega's.

"Hello," said Bellatrix. "I heard we have a visitor. May I help?"

Marcie looked over her shoulder at Bellatrix from where she stood up on the ladder. She blushed, and Altair was unsure if she was embarrassed to have been caught looking at the animals, afraid that she was in trouble, or if she found Bellatrix attractive too. Perhaps she was interested in more than male-shaped bodies.

"Sorry for the intrusion," said Marcie as she climbed down the ladder. "If I'm a bother, I can go."

"You may stay," said Bellatrix. She turned to Altair. "Are you giving your charge a tour?"

"Yes."

"Have you given her a tour of the android repair centre?"

"She was denied access."

"Understood."

When Marcie had her feet on the ground and had turned, Bellatrix asked, "Would you like a closer look at one?"

"Yes, please," said Marcie, her eyes wide and her shoulders raising. She bounced on her toes while Bellatrix moved to the familiar storage.

"What is your name?" asked Bellatrix.

"Marcie Martin-Palmer."

Altair knew what was coming if Bellatrix was asking for her name, and wondered what Vega would think. Would this not be a bigger security breach than letting Marcie into where the androids were fixed?

"Martin," said Bellatrix. "Yes, we have one in stock." She climbed the ladder to a small cubby, opened it, and carried down a blue speck.

Marcie looked quizzically at Altair.

"We match familiars to names if possible, to make it easier to remember who belongs to who," he said. "I have an eagle familiar because the star Altair was known in some old Earth cultures as the 'Eagle Star'."

"But..." said Marcie as she followed Bellatrix over to the workbench to look at the animal android. It was a small bird, its feathers mostly a bright blue that looked like it was not the natural plumage colour of the species it copied. The bird's belly was white.

Bellatrix waved a device over the bird, and it turned on, hopping up on its feet and letting out a high-pitched warbling. Bellatrix stepped back and brushed her long purple hair back over her shoulder. It seemed to be a calculatedly human gesture. "This is a house martin, of the genus *Delichon*," she said. "Please look the bird in the eye." Marcie did as she was told, if hesitantly. "Bonding protocol engaged," said Bellatrix, pressing a button on the device in her hand. "Please state your full name."

"Marcie Martin-Palmer."

"Please state a designation for your familiar."

Marcie said nothing for a moment. Then she glanced at Altair, gave a lop-sided smile, and said, "Delichon."

"Bonding protocol finished. Calibration protocol engaged. Your familiar will now say a series of words. Please repeat each one. Your familiar will also look at you from several angles."

Bellatrix stepped away as Delichon began saying a string of random words while hopping back and forth on the workbench. Marcie repeated each word, a big smile on her face. Altair followed Bellatrix so that he would be out of the way of the calibration protocol.

"Is this a good idea?" asked Altair in a voice too low for Marcie to hear.

"You have security concerns?"

"Perhaps."

"Your role is to entertain your guest for the benefit of our settlement. The humans could cause us trouble. It is in our best interests to keep them amused so that they think less about the gaps in our memories, what they could mean, and if we should be deactivated and packed away in boxes labelled 'hazardous goods'."

For once, Altair did not need to wonder what his fellow android was thinking. That was a very clear opinion.

"This human seems distracted by the cute animals. Therefore, this is an excellent idea. Keep it up."

"Keep it up, how?"

"Do what you're programmed to do, by whichever method seems like it will be most efficacious. Show her scenery, show her fancy gadgets, seduce her, ask her about herself. Humans love to talk about themselves. Or so I understand."

Altair gave Bellatrix a long look. Hers was a harsh world view. He wondered what her experience of the Event Horizon had been, what trauma she had awoken to. He wasn't the only one who had awoken damaged and afraid.

"What if the humans need to be protected against us?" he asked.

"What if they do? They have their own security staff. They will do their jobs. Yours is to make sure the humans leave here thinking of us favourably."

Altair looked at the bright smile on Marcie's face. It seemed Altair was doing his job just fine. But was he doing right by his guest in a moral sense?

CHAPTER 11

She was enamoured.

The small android Delichon sat on her shoulder as she prepared to leave the android engineering centre. It cheeped soothingly, its claws digging into her uniform. It was so *cute*. So *fluffy*. It's diminutive, whistling voice so *sweet*. Oh, she knew she was being distracted. They were uncomfortable with her seeing the rest of the centre. That was fine, because she had something important to report.

Colony 227C was a research colony. Therefore, there had to be a research centre in the settlement. Altair had given her a good rundown of what all the big buildings in the settlement were for, or what they had been for. The unused school and medical centre were particularly poignant; she'd had to work hard not to tear up at their mention. But the only building that could have been the actual research location was the android engineering building. Therefore, 227C had been an *android* research centre. Hence the amazingly detailed animal work. Hence the amazingly detailed *person* work. Hence why the androids here had somehow thrived for 29 years as individuals. And maybe that was a major clue about what had happened to the humans.

They would all have to be wary around the androids, just in case. This may not have been another Hellas Basin incident, but something strange had happened.

"Would you like to see something else now?" asked Altair as they left the building.

"Sure. How about that beach?" She could pretend like she only had leisure on her mind now. She still intended to ask Altair some questions, though.

"This way, please."

They began to walk, but then Hieraaetus swooped down to sit on Altair's shoulder. "Shaula requests you wait a moment," it said in its croaky, raven-like voice.

"Understood."

Marcie waited with Altair as he stood outside the centre. Hieraaetus and Delichon looked at each other from their respective shoulders as they waited. Delichon chirruped, and Hieraaetus responded in a deeper bird voice. Maybe she was imagining it, but it seemed the birds were introducing themselves to each other. Soon a green female android, smaller than many of the others around, but still taller than Marcie and perfectly formed, strode out the front door.

"Altair, please explain yourself," she said.

Altair cocked his head at the other android, presumably this Shaula who had asked him to wait. "Explain what, may I ask?"

"Why you brought a human here." Her face was hard. Well, all the androids had faces that could be described as hard, but this android's face had a different kind of hardness. This was something to do with how she had individuated.

"Excuse me," said Marcie, not wanting Altair to get in trouble for her sake. "I requested a tour, and when we were told where I was not welcome, Altair only took me to the animal room."

Shaula looked at Marcie for the first time. "You expect me to believe you were not looking for information in my clinic?"

"No," said Marcie. "Of course I was; we would be fools not to at least look into what happened here. But I've no intention of going behind anyone's back to get that information."

Shaula stared at her for an uncomfortably long time. Then she looked at Delichon, who still sat on Marcie's shoulder. "I see Bellatrix at least was with you."

"Yes," said Marcie. "If it's a problem that I have this little one, let me know."

"At least this human will be easier than the others to locate," she said to Altair. She turned and walked back to the centre. "Don't exceed your designation, Altair."

"Well," said Marcie after she was gone. "I had to annoy someone. I always annoy someone. Shall we go to the beach?"

Altair led her along a different road, one that ran parallel to the shore. A row of those aged temporary shelter huts ran along it on the landward side. At the far end of the row, two different houses stood alone. There had probably originally been huts there too, but they had been replaced with proper two-storey houses at some point, houses with large electrofilm windows looking out over the lake. The view and breezes must be phenomenal from inside. Beside the two good houses was an empty lot, full of weeds, the same size as the lots that the huts stood on.

Marcie pointed at the houses. "Were those there at your Event Horizon?" That's what he had referred to the beginning of his memory as, wasn't it?

"Yes. The farthest house had signs of habitation. The next one was completed but contained no belongings. The bare lot next door had a round cleared patch. We believe a temporary hut had just been cleared to make room for another permanent dwelling shortly before the humans left."

"The settlement must have been so new when things went wrong," said Marcie. "A few years at most, maybe?" All the hope that the colonists must have held, all to be dashed away. No one made buildings like the Welcome Centre or that fancy inventory warehouse lightly. The people had meant to stay.

"We believe so, too."

"Are you looking for what happened?"

"We want to, of course. But we have exhausted our leads."

"Perhaps we can help once our ship is fixed. There might be a satellite or something with data that you haven't been able to access."

Altair looked as if he was going to respond, but then he held out a hand and pointed to a beach access that crossed over the top of a small dune.

Marcie walked ahead of him over the sand-blasted boards and onto the brown sand and pebble beach. It was no sea beach, but it was respectable for a lake.

Marcie picked her way over to a weathered piece of driftwood, something long and straight, a young tree lost to rough weather, perhaps. There were no old, twisted trees on 227C yet. It hadn't been long enough since the terraforming process for the ecosystem to age up. She sat on the driftwood, checked that Delichon still had a good perch on her shoulder, and then picked up a handful of sand and gravel. It differed from Earth sand, but was like the sand she'd seen on many other terraformed colonies. Earth's sand was awash with the remains of life, the pieces within often the weathered and crumbled detritus of long dead animals and plants. But the sand of these colonies was usually just rock fragments with only the odd new speck of life: a stray twig fragment, a shattered beetle carapace. If you looked closely enough, the difference was clear.

Marcie viewed the shimmering water. The lake was broad; the hills on the far shore were distant and faded by haze even on this sunny day. Though the sand was different, the waters still lapped against the shore in a comforting murmur, just like Earth lakes did. Physics was still physics, no matter where you went. Marcie took that knowledge with her like a comforting blanket wherever she ventured with the Orion Navy.

Marcie looked for Altair, the most obvious reminder on the beach of where she was. He stood about ten paces away, Hieraaetus still on his shoulder, keeping himself behind her. Both Altair and his familiar looked in her direction. Was he trying not to disturb her view of the sparking lake? Or just keeping a wary eye on her?

Altair's hair blew in the unimpeded lake breeze, his smart, crisp haircut not sharp enough to avoid being mussed by the weather. He looked like he ought to be wearing a smart suit and polished shoes, with a tie flapping in the breeze, not... nothing.

Marcie waved him over. "Join me. You loom when you stand like that."

He walked over, leaving deep footprints in the sand. "Stand like what?"

"In a looming sort of manner."

"If you are referring to my height, I am afraid the only accommodation I can make is to take a seat." He folded down, down, and perched on the driftwood. She had hoped that he'd sit with his knees up, hiding the more obvious nakedness of his body, but he instead settled into a cross-legged position, his knees down on the sand, and let it all hang out. Hieraaetus elected to take flight and swoop in circles far above them.

Marcie wondered for a minute how to approach getting information from Altair. As accommodating as he'd been, he clearly had orders to keep everything surface-level only. What she'd got out of him the night before may have been a fluke. And she needed to dig deeper yet. "Tell me about your own impressions of the colony."

"My impressions?"

"Yes; how do you feel about this settlement?"

"The climate and terrain are conducive to food production and a pleasant existence for biotic life."

"I mean, the settlement as a community."

Altair tilted his head. "That is difficult to say. We are not a community in the normal sense."

Marcie frowned. "Who said?"

"It is only logical that we are not."

Marcie shook her head. "I don't agree. If you're individuating, then you're a community of individuals like any other."

Altair thought about her words for a long moment. "Then perhaps we are a community that bears the burden of a trauma."

Marcie didn't push further on that topic, because the fact that he'd described the mystery of their past as a 'trauma' told her much about the colony and how they had fared over the last 29 years. "Tell me about yourself," she said instead. She was consciously keeping her sentences short and direct so as not to overwhelm or confuse him with the normal filler and blather of human conversation.

"What do you want to know?"

"Anything you think is relevant."

He thought for longer this time. "You seem like a nice person," he said, a surprising non sequitur for an android. "May I ask you to listen without jumping to conclusions?"

Marcie's heart rate increased. Finally, she was getting somewhere. "Sure. Of course."

"I am afraid sometimes."

Marcie felt a chill. Even though she had figured out the androids were individuating, it was still bizarre to hear an android admit to experiencing fear. "Afraid of what?"

"I am not sure. As far as I am aware, the memories and knowledge that were deleted in the Event Horizon are lost to me forever. And yet, something seems to linger within me. Something that makes me aware there is a lack."

"A lack of knowledge."

"Yes, but it is a fundamental lack, not merely the missing information from our memories and databases. Something was wrong here. Maybe it still is. But we do not know what." He looked into her eyes. "I cannot be 100% certain that you are safe here, Marcie Martin-Palmer. I wish I could be, but I am not."

Marcie gave him a crooked smile. "We're officers of the Orion Navy, trained for danger. We didn't come here expecting a 100% chance of being safe. There's a reason we get hazard pay for missions like this." She looked out over the rippling lake surface. "If something happens here, and I'm injured, it wouldn't be the first time since taking up my commission."

"You have a contusion on your cheek."

"Exactly. I got this bruise when our ship was damaged. Hit my face on my workstation. It's fine. I expect stuff like this."

Altair gazed at the far shore. "I cannot even promise you are safe in my presence. I think you are, but I do not know what lurks within my code that has been wiped from my memory."

"I feel safe with you. You swore an oath to do me no harm, and you showed me how to use the alert on your charging station."

"I did. However, you slept through that alarm this morning. I was out in the apartment before you awoke."

Marcie's lips twisted at the memory of her sharp stab of panic that morning. "True. I'll sleep lighter tonight, I promise."

"Thank you. That is all I ask — that you do not take your safety in my presence for granted."

Altair stilled and looked at the lake some more, as movable as a statue. Marcie looked at him for a long moment, looking for any hint of his thoughts, but of course, he was not human. She couldn't read him.

"In my experience," she said as she fussed with Delichon and handed it down from her shoulder to the sand, "anyone who worries about their impact on others and thinks they're not safe or good to be around is probably good. The terrors of this galaxy fully believe that they're justified in whatever they do, and in no need of self-reflection. Anyone who reflects as much as you do is doing fine."

He looked at her again and quirked a perfect eyebrow, a gesture that was utterly smooth, as if copied from a programmed routine. As it probably was. "I had not considered my worries from that angle."

"People usually don't until someone else reminds them to."

"You are very philosophical for a human. Tell me more about yourself."

Marcie recognised a purposeful change of topic when she heard one, but she let him turn the conversation, nonetheless. How he reacted to her might be illuminating too. "There's not much to say," she said, as she watched Delichon peck about in the sand as if mimicking a real bird, and pausing now and then to look around with a more android-like mien. "I'm from England, which is part of the New European Union on Earth. I studied engineering at university, but then when I found it hard to get a civilian job, because there are so many graduates these days, I signed up to the Orion Navy Academy, graduated, got a placement on a ship as an ensign, and I've been working my way up ever since."

"Do you have family?"

"Parents in the Midlands; that's part of England. My Mum was once a ship's engineer too. I have... had..." She sighed and picked Delichon up again, getting it to perch on her finger. "I've been through a breakup."

"What is a breakup?"

Marcie snorted. Of course: knowledge gaps. "I had a romantic partner, but she sent me a communication saying she no longer wished to be in a relationship with me."

"Ah," said Altair. "My apologies for asking about a difficult topic."

"No, it's fine."

"Your sexual preference is for women?"

"*Now* you're being too nosey."

"My apologies. It is not a topic that I need to inquire about."

"Too right."

"Since you blush when you look at my body."

Marcie spluttered. "Excuse *you*. You can't just say that! Aren't you a polite android?"

"My apologies. I seem to have encountered a gap in my programming regarding human interaction. Recalibrating."

"Good. You do that."

"Do you like being an engineer?" he asked, as if he had never brought up the previous topic.

Marcie had whiplash. "Yeah, I do. I like it a lot. I enjoy figuring out solutions to problems, fixing things that others can't. You know, noodling away at a problem until I crack it."

Before Altair could ask another question, Hieraaetus swooped down and landed on the driftwood beside him. "Humans of the landing party are approaching. They have left their hosts behind."

Altair and Marcie looked at one another. Hieraaetus's description of the approaching situation was simple, and yet Marcie had a bad feeling.

"Thank you, Hieraaetus," said Altair. "Please observe and record our interaction with them if they come here."

Marcie nodded at him. Yes, that was a good idea. Particularly if the approaching human was Sub Lieutenant Gagnon.

CHAPTER 12

Altair stood up to watch the approaching humans. Behind him, Marcie also stood.

Three humans approached: the other members of the visiting party except for the commander. Their hosts did not accompany them. Altair wondered why not.

The humans did not appear to have known that Marcie and Altair would be on the beach. The woman with the orange hair saw them first and her posture stiffened. A moment later, the two men caught sight of them, and both stopped.

Marcie walked past Altair towards her crew mates, Delichon following her and settling on her shoulder. She waved and approached them. Soon, the humans held a whispered discussion.

Altair did not like the development. The humans should have been with their hosts, for several reasons. Also, he would be seen in dereliction of duty if he did not intervene. He approached the group, aware of Hieraaetus circling above.

"Good morning," he said to the approaching group. "May I help you? Are you looking for your hosts? They should be attending to you."

All the humans looked at him and fell silent.

"We're just taking a bit of a walk before lunch, is all," said the security lieutenant. "Your fellows know where we are."

There was something blank about the faces of the three newly arrived humans, something that, were they androids, would have prompted him to wish, as he often did, that the network was still active. But Marcie's face and body language were more mobile. Her features twisted, and she shifted on her feet. She was a bell-weather for the discomfort the other humans must be feeling in his presence.

"Understood. I shall not interrupt your walk." After all, Hieraaetus was keeping a watchful eye over all. Altair stepped several paces away to give the humans a semblance of privacy and waited.

The orange-haired woman snorted. The darker-skinned man looked down at his own feet.

Marcie cleared her throat. "I won't keep you, either," she said to her fellow humans. "I'll see you back at the Welcome Centre for lunch."

"You're going to stay with that thing?" asked the orange-haired woman. "Still finding it 'amiable'?"

Marcie stood taller. "Yes," she said, though she also made a slight movement with her head and a shrug with her shoulder. Perhaps a covert attempt at communicating something to the humans and not to himself?

"Ah," said Altair after a quick analysis of probabilities. "You are signalling to your crew mates you are still on your information-gathering exercise."

Marcie's cheeks coloured pink, and the security human let out a burbling laugh. "You told him?"

"He figured it out," said Marcie. "And why bother denying it? It's only logical."

"Indeed," said Altair. "I would think less of you if you did not display curiosity about the unusual circumstances in this colony." Altair paused a moment before continuing. He had something he wanted the humans other than Marcie to hear that he was not sure other androids would be keen for him to say. But it needed to be said. "Our colony has exhausted our means of investigating the past. Fresh eyes and new methodologies are welcome, and much needed."

"What does that mean?" muttered the darker-skinned man. But he was still looking down, so Altair allocated the utterance the status of a rhetorical question.

"Whatever," said the red-haired woman. "What on Earth is that thing on your shoulder?" She pointed at Delichon.

"We're not on Earth, we're on 227C," said Marcie. "And it's one of the animal androids. I visited the android engineering centre earlier."

"Is that safe?" asked the security person.

Marcie shrugged. "It seems programmable, as in it'll be as safe as I encourage it to be. And it's interesting."

The orange-haired woman's lip curled. "*Engineers*," she said, with such a heavy loading of contempt that Altair identified it easily.

He looked at Marcie. He wondered how the small human woman would deal with such hostility from her own kind. Would she be emotionally wounded? But no. She drew her shoulders back. "Sub Lieutenant Gagnon, you're out of line. I'm pursuing my mission on 227C, as appropriately as I can, while causing as little trouble as I can. Can you say the same?"

Interestingly, the sub lieutenant also stood straight. "My apologies, lieutenant, sir."

"You're dismissed," said Marcie. "I'll see you later. Please don't be concerned. Everything here is under control."

"Listen to the lieutenant," said the security person. "Or I'll label you as a hindrance to the mission myself." He shepherded his two fellows away. As they left, he gave Marcie a thumbs-up over his shoulder.

Once they were back over the dune, Marcie sighed and slumped. "Sorry about that, Altair."

Altair did not need the apology, but he appreciated it nonetheless. "Different humans of your party treat me in different ways."

"Yes. People have different feelings about androids based on their upbringing and previous life experiences. Also, the attitudes in the places where they grew up. People from Hellas Basin, for example."

"Hellas Basin?" Altair consulted his databanks. "Is that a place on the planet Mars?"

Marcie gave him a long look. "Never mind. It's not a cheery topic. Perhaps we can leave it for another day." She took a deep breath. "Can we walk along the beach for a bit before I go back for lunch?"

"Of course."

He walked behind her and observed her as she walked. She was asking Delichon questions, working out what she could of its programming. She was an interesting being, Marcie Martin-Palmer. Small and delicate-seeming, but strong-willed. Intelligent and knowledgeable. More accepting of Altair than any of the other humans. But... damaged. Sad. The hostility of one crew mate may have contributed, but also her 'breakup'.

Altair's role as host extended beyond looking after basic needs such as accommodation, food, and guidance. He was also expected, by the protocols left to him, to take care of a visitor's emotional needs as well, if he deemed it necessary. He was beginning to appreciate

Marcie for seeing who he was better than most. Was there anything he could do to help her as a token of his appreciation?

He almost stopped walking in surprise. He sought... a personal connection with the visiting human? Was that wise? But there was a whisper in his subroutines, a ghost in his code. *Why not?*

CHAPTER 13

Marcie didn't like being judged. All afternoon, however, the feeling lingered. She held in her indignation. She had been assigned to gather information! Of course she had gone on a tour with her host alone! It made sense.

Though, Marcie wondered if it was not Altair, but Delichon, that had made Gagnon act so strange, and Fisher follow suit, and O'Donoghue look at her with inscrutable thoughts. Was it strange that she had accepted the animal messenger? It was only for a day. But of course, the small bird could have been programmed to spy on them. Of course, Marcie knew that. But she figured it didn't matter, in amongst all the other opportunities to monitor them that the androids had. What was one more android bird flitting about and monitoring Marcie?

After lunch, Marcie updated Commander Mori on what she had learned, that 227C had most likely been an android research and development centre, and that the one thing the androids were most protective of was the android repair centre.

The commander nodded along, and said, "Thank you, lieutenant. Good work."

Then Marcie spent a portion of the afternoon sitting outside on a bench seat in the dappled shade of a tree, the scent of rose and jasmine around her, and wrote a report to engineering on her tablet. It was a dry report about the parts she was expecting to be bringing home the next day and the workarounds that would be needed to install them. Her attention wandered. Sometimes she petted Delichon, or watched it flying around the garden, or swooping up to confer with Hieraaetus, who often sat perched on the roof edge. But often, her attention was drawn to Altair.

He spent most of the time sitting on another bench, not looking in her direction at all. A few times, he stood and pulled a few weeds he spotted in the garden. Once, Hieraaetus swooped down and the two androids, humanoid and avian, had a quick conversation.

But most of the time, he just sat there, and Marcie's attention kept returning to him whenever her concentration slipped. Not just because he was an impressive sight with that perfect frame and excellent muscular sculpting. It had been pleasant going on the tour with him that morning. It worried her. Was Gagnon right? Was she too quick to get comfortable around these androids, because she was an engineer and her brain was wired differently? Was she being unwise?

But, hell, anyone could be dangerous. There were many dangerous humans around, particularly the space pirates who kept hitting the trade lanes. What was the damned difference? Especially since these androids on this colony were individuating. They were people now.

Right?

Marcie finally finished her report and hit 'send'. She figured Ife would read it soon; Simons delegated things like that to Marcie first, and Ife second. She waved the thought of Simons away. She'd accepted this assignment so that she wouldn't have to think of him for a few days!

Marcie stood and stretched out the kinks in her back. Altair, who had been paying her more attention than he pretended to, stood as well. Marcie walked over to him. "I'm tired. There's more gravity here than I've felt in months, and it's wearing on me. I'm going to go up to the room to rest."

"I will accompany you there," said Altair. "If you like, I could use the recharge station so that you have some privacy."

Marcie gave a crooked smile. It seemed he was both trying to follow his orders and be considerate at the same time. She appreciated the compromise.

They went up to the suite together. "Do you require anything?" asked Altair.

"No, thank you. I think I'm just going to take a nap before dinner."

"Understood. Please press the summon button if you need me." He stepped into his recharge station.

The suite felt bigger when Marcie was alone. She sighed and went to the kitchenette. On the bench, she found a small bundle of fresh-picked daisies. Delichon hopped down off her shoulder and sat beside the daisies. "Chamomile," it said in its fluting voice. "Please steep in water to make a relaxing and restful infusion."

"Thank you. Please recharge if you like."

Delichon flitted over to Hieraaetus's perch and put one wing over the side of its head to sleep.

Marcie had never made a tisane from fresh flowers before. She eyed the recharge station. When had Altair organised this? When he talked to Hieraaetus in the garden?

She did her best to brew a drink from the flowers, and then she took the drink to the sofa. It wasn't the same as drinking chamomile tea made from dried flowers, but it wasn't unpleasant either. If anything, it was nicer. Who would have known?

She nursed her beverage and enjoyed the refreshing breeze and the way it played with the sheer curtains. Then she washed her cup in the sink and went to the bedroom to attempt a nap.

It didn't work, despite the chamomile. Her thoughts kept turning over and over. It seemed she hadn't yet processed the damage to the *Sunda Tiger*, because that harrowing minute after impact kept playing in her mind. Also, the judgemental look she'd seen on Gagnon's face that morning. She imagined the look on the faces of all the rest of her crew. It was as if everyone were looking at her and thinking she was disgusting.

Too cruel, brain, she thought. *Lay off! Why would my crew all suddenly turn against me, just because I accepted the company of a small android bird for a day?*

But, the realisation came to her, that's not what she was anxious about. If anyone had seen the way Marcie had talked with Altair about her insecurities, about how he'd talked about some of his own... If they had seen the way she couldn't keep her eyes off his form...

She jumped up and went to the bathroom, intending to distract herself with a shower. A *cool* one. Her thoughts, though, were scattering like spooked cats, utterly unherdable. She had *looked*, she had *looked a lot*. Had it been that long since she got laid? Of course it was. Even the last time she was back in London with Lisa, they hadn't quite... Well, perhaps the writing had been on the wall for her relationship even then and she just hadn't paid attention. And now she was so desperate she was being charmed by a naked blue android who was programmed to have good manners and be considerate. *For goodness' sake, Marcie! Get a grip!*

How was she going to face her crew mates over dinner after this realisation? How was she going to face Altair?

CHAPTER 14

Red arms. Blackened hands.

Who am I?

What have I done?

What is that beeping?

With a start, Altair remembered his current task. The beeping noise was a summons. Marcie needed him.

Altair stumbled out of the recharge station, checking his internal chronometer. The time surprised him. It was dinnertime. He did not like how The Memory made him lose his bearings.

"Hell—oh! Are you all right?" Marcie reached out and gripped his forearm. Altair looked down into her pink face, perhaps freshly scrubbed in the shower. Her eyes were wide and her mouth hung open.

She can see The Memory lingering about me. How do humans sense such things?

"I am fine, Marcie," he said. "I neglected to take a moment to regain my bearings."

She let go of his arm and nodded. "I'm sorry I've taken your bed. I know you rarely use that cubby."

"It is all right."

"Yeah, I'll be out of your way soon." She dropped her gaze to the floor. She seemed more disturbed than before.

"Are you all right?" he asked her. "Was your nap refreshing?"

She wrapped one arm around herself and held onto the opposite elbow. "Um, no. Not really. I don't feel so good. Would it be OK if I ate dinner in the suite this evening? I've already told my colleagues I'm not feeling great, that the gravity and warmth are getting to me."

"Of course," said Altair. "I will go fetch your meal."

Altair left the suite, wondering if he should trust Marcie's own assessment of the cause of her malaise, or if he should ask one of the medical androids to attend her. He decided she would know better than him how a planet would affect her after a lengthy journey on a ship.

Vega waylaid him on the way to the kitchens. "Altair, I need a debrief."

"I can spare a minute," said Altair, "though I am currently running an errand for my charge."

Vega looked around again, verifying that they were alone. "I want a report of what you have seen and heard."

If Altair were human, he may have sighed. This did not need to be a meeting. It could have been a simple message run via Hieraaetus. "I have already submitted a report about the security system ping. Did you receive it?"

"Yes."

"I have nothing further to add to the report."

"You took your human charge on a tour of the settlement. Did anything come of that tour?"

"Nothing of note. Lieutenant Martin-Palmer complied with good grace when denied access to the android repair centre. She admitted to being on a fact-finding mission, but such a mission is understandable considering how little the humans know of us. Some of the other humans seemed mistrustful of me, but I believe this also to be within acceptable tolerance. We must expect caution from the humans."

"Any evidence of unacceptable activities or intentions for sabotage?"

"None. I have seen no evidence of the humans having any motives other than those they have outwardly stated."

Vega stood still for a moment. "Acknowledged," he finally said. "Keep me informed." He strode out of the Welcome Centre.

Altair put Vega's suspicions out of mind and went to the kitchen. He loaded Marcie's plate with the foods she had eaten the day before, and not the ones she had tried and put aside. Then he took the meal up to the suite and put it on the table for her. "Shall I stay awake while you eat in case you would like me to get something more for you from the kitchen, or would you like some privacy again?" he asked.

"Oh, um," said Marcie as she fished in a drawer for cutlery. "Uh, stay awake, I guess? I don't want to force you to stay in that little cubby just for my sake."

Altair took a seat on the sofa while Marcie ate her dinner. He took the time to ponder the puzzle that was Marcie, here in this space, in this time, in this situation. The arrival of humans had not been unexpected, but it had been surprising. Until Marcie had been assigned to him, he had been concerned about hosting a human when he had not yet untangled his own past and discovered what happened before the Event Horizon. But that day, when they had talked, Altair had finally appreciated that, as a human, Marcie understood the untidiness that came from a life of imperfect conditions.

But she would leave tomorrow. Perhaps permanently.

Altair had been concerned about being in close proximity to a human. But now, he was growing concerned about her leaving. None of his fellow androids seemed to have the anxieties he had. Or, if they did, they did not express them in the same way. They did not understand him, because their individual codes left them little room to adapt. Marcie was a human, with innate adaptability, and she seemed to regard him with friendliness. He did not know if any of the other humans of the team could see him that way. If any other humans could. He had not yet debriefed the other hosts and discussed their interactions with their own charges.

It might just be Marcie.

He might only have these next few hours to... to what?

To connect with someone who sympathised.

Marcie finished her meal and took her plate and cutlery to the sink. A sense of urgency took a hold of Altair. "May I speak with you?" he asked.

"Um, sure." Marcie sat on the other length of the sofa, her knees together with her hands resting on them and her back straight. She didn't look directly at him. "What would you like to speak about?"

Altair paused. "I am not sure how to proceed. I am concerned I will not use the right words and express myself poorly."

Marcie leaned forward. "Take your time."

He gazed at Marcie, trying to decide on his strategy for the conversation. The contusion on Marcie's face was already changing colour. It had been purple, but now the bruise was greenish around the edges. Humans were so changeable, the details about them mutable on short time scales. Androids were unchanging. Altair was supposed to stay the same, never need more than he had.

But he was not what he was supposed to be.

"In your professional opinion as an engineer, is it possible for individuating androids to develop what could be considered colloquially as 'emotional needs'?"

Marcie's eyebrows rose. "Uh, hm. I don't know. Do you think you have emotional needs?"

"Something is missing," he said. "Other than my memories, of course."

Marcie rubbed a hand over her head. "There's something in human psychology called Maslow's Human Needs. The theory goes that a person must have all of their needs met, or they'll be off-balance and develop insecurities and behaviour problems."

Altair consulted his database, but this category of human psychology was not covered. "What are the needs?"

"They form a hierarchy. The needs towards the bottom are most fundamental and must be met first. They go something like physiological needs, safety, love and belonging, self-actualisation... no, next is esteem, then self-actualisation. So someone who is living in poverty can have trouble with the bottom tier, and someone who is not understood by society and shunned might have trouble with the esteem tier..."

"And someone who has just suffered the end of a relationship might have trouble with the love and belonging tier?"

She wrinkled her nose. "Uh, *ouch*. But yes, you get the idea."

"My apologies."

"Anyway, perhaps there could be some parallel set of needs for androids, which ought to be mapped out? And if you're individuating, many of the tiers might even be similar."

Altair gazed out the electrofilm window at the orange and pink sunset. "The needs as you describe them make sense to me. Perhaps what constitutes them changes? For example, my physiological needs include a charging station and access to the android repair centre when I damage my silicone skin."

Marcie nodded. "And your safety needs would include a safe network and safe access to data. Look, right there, a safety need not being met."

"Love and belonging, though... they are not something that androids are supposed to need."

"Except I think you do. Now."

Altair looked at her, and at the sunset reflected in her eyes. "You think so?"

"I haven't seen you talking to many other androids while I've been here."

"I have been busy."

"It looks like you usually are. In the garden. Not with other androids. Perhaps what you're missing is companionship. You were programmed to be networked with your fellows, but you're not. Maybe you were just never taught how to put in the hard work."

"The hard work?"

She grinned at him. "What we're doing now. Talking. Forming connections the old-fashioned way."

The more he thought about it, the more he realised she was right. He had spent 28 years, 7 months, and 22 days wishing he was still networked with his fellow androids so he could know what they were thinking. All along, he could have just *asked* them. It was a fundamental shift in his perspective. "I have wished I was still networked so I could know what the others were thinking 14,107 times, and now you make me realise each one of those wishes was a wasted opportunity to become something more than I was programmed to be."

She laughed. "That's an accurate count, isn't it?"

"Of course."

"Well, no one left you a blueprint of how to proceed without humans or a network. Of course it was difficult."

"Thank you for understanding."

"No problem. So, what about esteem?"

"Perhaps every single android in the settlement has trouble with esteem. None of us are sure that the roles we were assigned after the Event Horizon were the ones we held before. We do not know for sure that we are in the right place."

"That's something else that could be helped with communication. Perhaps you need to have a town meeting where you compare data and observations from the last 29 years and see if anyone could be reassigned for a better fit."

He nodded. "I will suggest such an approach to Sirius."

"And self-actualisation?" she asked, shifting her position to cross her legs.

"I do not know what that looks like in practice. But..." he paused, not sure if he should confide his secret in her.

"But...?" she prompted.

It was the last night before she left. He would not have another chance. And she had been so helpful so far. "I do not think I can have self-actualisation without my lost memories."

"Isn't who you are now enough?"

He shook his head. "I wish it was, but... I cannot be sure that I did not have a role to play in the disappearance of the humans. Because I cannot remember, I do not know if I did something... bad."

She frowned. "Do you have a reason to think you did?"

He clasped his hands together and looked down at them. While they talked, the hue of the sunset had shifted and seemed to paint his skin red. He stood up and walked over to the control panel to turn on all the lights in the suite. Still facing the wall, he said, "I awoke from the Event Horizon with blackened, charred hands."

He heard a sharp inhalation behind him. "And you think that means you were involved?"

"I do not know for sure, but..."

"You could have been trying to *save* people. There's no way to know either way."

"Then why do I always see those hands in a nightmare?" He blinked. He'd never used that word to refer to The Memory. It was far too human a word.

"Come here," said Marcie.

He turned around to see her patting the seat beside her. He did as she bid and sat beside her on the sofa. She reached out and took a hold of his closest hand, turning it over in her own, inspecting it from all angles.

"If I didn't already know you were individuating, I would know it now. I may not be getting the same physiological cues from you I'd get from a human, but you're clearly terrified."

"Terror is a human emotion."

"One you share." She looked up into his eyes. "I can't wipe that terror from your mind. All I can do is remind you that the history you fear is only one possibility. Put it aside for now, and only deal with it when you regain your memories."

"If."

"When."

"How can you reassure me like this? What if you are not safe with me, Marcie? What if something triggers—?"

"Hush," she said, and gave his hand a squeeze. "I'm a small woman, not very strong physically. I'm not truly safe with *any*one. I can never know what lurks at the bottom of another's soul. You're no different."

"How do you continue to interact with others calmly, with those sorts of thoughts?"

"I just cross my fingers and hope for the best. Like everyone else in this universe."

And, somehow, the conversation had gone full-circle, to where he wondered if it would, could go. "Can you teach me?"

"How to hope for the best?"

"Yes. And how to reach out, and make connections, and help others meet their needs while also meeting my own?"

She blushed and gulped. "Uh, um..." She stared up into his eyes, her own irises seeming a deeper blue than usual. She laughed nervously. "You mean talk some more? More heart-to-heart?"

"Some of that, yes," said Altair. "But as discussed earlier, your needs have been compromised by the end of a relationship. I'm offering to assist you with those needs in return for the immense help you have offered me this evening."

"Belonging?"

"In the way of an evening of companionship. But my understanding of human physiology indicates the end of a relationship may lead to physiological needs also remaining unmet."

Marcie gulped. But there was still a furrow between her brows, still a question in her eyes.

He needed to be more clear. "By which," he said, "I am offering you sexual intercourse."

CHAPTER 15

Marcie jumped to her feet. She thought she'd been imagining things at first, but she wasn't. Altair was hitting on her. He was really hitting on her! "Uh, um, oh."

"I have shocked you," he said. "Was I too blunt?"

"Very, very blunt. So blunt. Um, why?"

Altair looked up at her patiently. "Because I wish to. Because it is an optional consideration of my hosting duties. Because you leave tomorrow, and tonight is all we have."

The last point was poetic, but she put that thought aside for the moment. "An optional consideration of your duties? As in, it's your job to 'service' me in such a way?"

He paused. "You seem irate. I have stumbled into a cultural misunderstanding."

"It sounds like a chore to you."

"That is not what I meant. Rather, it is my job to consider the emotional and physical needs of my charges. But I have broad latitude in how I serve those needs. Intimacy is pre-approved."

Marcie took a couple of steadying breaths. Perhaps she had over-reacted. But also, this all felt so strange.

"I am programmed in multiple methods of giving pleasure."

At the word 'programmed,' it was as if an entire bucket of ice water had been dumped over her ardour. Marcie sat on the sofa again, this time not as close to Altair as before. "Look, Altair, I appreciate the offer, but if this is something you've been programmed to offer, then I have questions about consent on your behalf. I don't want to take advantage of you."

As still as he usually was, Marcie could tell he was suddenly frozen.

"Uh, my turn to stumble into a cultural misunderstanding?" she asked.

"Marcie," said Altair. "I thought you saw me more like a person than your crew mates do."

Marcie raised her hands. "I do, honest! But I have concerns about how programming interferes with these sorts of things. The concept of consent is important to me."

He turned to face her more directly. "You speak as if there are shades of meaning here, but there are not. This is a binary issue. Either I am a person, and my verbal consent is sufficient, because I can make my own decisions. Or, I am nothing but a machine. Either way, your ability to have intercourse with me without qualms is assured. Because either I am a man, or I am a sex toy."

"Oh Altair, I didn't mean..."

"I see you did not. But it is the logical endpoint of that thought process. Because I have batteries and I can stay as hard as you need me to."

"Oh, Altair, I—"

"And I vibrate."

Marcie bit her lip. Her stomach flipped. "...Vibrate?"

"And I have fine temperature control."

"Uh." It was suddenly stifling in the apartment. *Oh God, what's wrong with me? Am I a bad person for being so tempted?*

Altair shifted closer on the sofa. "Merely give your assent, and we can spend a little time together in a closer manner. I learn more about how to be an individual, and you feel some physical pleasures you have been going without."

Marcie looked at his perfectly sculpted lips and licked her own in response. "I'm going to the special hell," she whispered to herself.

"Pardon? I have no context for that statement."

"I mean, yes."

Altair took no time to consider her acceptance. He raised a hand to the back of her neck, tipped her head, and bent down to give her a gentle kiss. He eased his lips over hers and moved with aching slowness, brushing her jaw with his other hand. Marcie, for the moment, sat still and let it happen. She could never keep her eyes open when she kissed. Her sight of him interrupted, she couldn't even tell the difference between being kissed by a human and an android. He was as warm and soft as if he were flesh and blood.

He leaned further into her and opened his lips, flicked his tongue out. Then she did feel a difference. He wasn't dry in his mouth, but the water in there, generated for her benefit, wasn't as slick as human saliva. She opened her mouth wide and slipped her tongue deep into his mouth, sharing her saliva with him until the feeling was right.

Whatever programming he possessed was impressive. He tangled his tongue with hers just right, dragged his fingers through her hair just right, slid his hand down to cup her breast just right. She let her own hands wander up his sculpted chest, over his shoulders, into his silky hair. Wherever her fingers travelled, she brushed the scent of him into the air: electric ozone, rather than the skin and musk of a human. He smelled like the environments she was most comfortable in.

She pulled back. “The electrofilm window is in privacy mode, right?”

“I made sure of it.”

“Planning all along to seduce me, huh?”

“I decided I would when we were walking on the beach.”

She looked up into his purple eyes. “Really?”

“Yes.” He emphasised the word with a tweak of her nipple through her uniform.

Marcie moaned and pulled him down for another lingering kiss. His chest heaved against her, dragging in deep breaths. He hadn’t shown signs of breathing before. Part of the programming, to make him feel more real against her?

Heat stifled Marcie, and she couldn’t handle her uniform anymore. She wormed her hand up between their bodies and tugged at the fastener.

“Allow me.” He held her by the hips and lifted her to stand in front of him between his knees. Marcie grabbed his shoulders, not sure that her knees were going to hold. She watched as he slid the fastener down and peeled her uniform off, revealing her bra. As hot as she was, her skin pebbled against the evening air.

Her uniform clung to her hips as Altair freed her arms from her sleeves. He ran one finger down her right biceps. “There is a mark here.”

“A scar from when I fell off a bike as a kid.”

“You did not have it patched. I thought humans could heal scars with modern medicine.”

“I decided to keep it as a reminder to be more careful. My parents let me.”

"Interesting." Altair leaned forward from his sitting position and kissed the scar.

"You don't think it's weird or ugly?"

"No, because it is yours."

Oh, he was *good.*

Altair pushed her uniform and underwear down over her hips and to her knees. She let her eyes roam over his body more openly than she'd ever done before. His broad shoulders, his muscled torso. His penis still was flaccid, which for a moment made Marcie wonder if he wasn't into it. But of course, he wasn't human. It wasn't fair to compare his reactions with a human man. 'Arousal' probably wasn't even a part of sex for him. But he'd said he wanted this, and she chose to believe him.

Altair leaned forward and lifted her right calf. She braced herself against him and let him carefully slip the leg of her uniform and her sock over her foot. He placed her bare foot down and repeated the process for the other leg. Finally, she unhooked her bra and tossed it aside, and stood before him naked. It was a big deal for her because she hadn't been naked in front of anyone for a while, but it was surely no big deal for him.

Altair rested his arm along the back of the sofa. He looked up at her, his face at rest, and watched her, waiting.

Waiting the see if she was still willing.

She really was.

Altair must have seen some affirmation in her face because, as if turned on with a switch, his penis came to life and rose to attention. It even had imitation throbbing veins. He had definitely been designed by some horny-on-main engineer. Marcie licked her lips while enjoying the view, then she straddled his lap.

"Is this OK?" she asked.

"Of course," he said, and placed his hands on her hips.

She stroked his chest again, then his stomach, then hovered her hands. "May I touch you there?"

"Yes."

She ran her fingers over his shaft. Just like his lips, he felt human. He was hot, throbbing, and silky, and the thin silicone skin slid over the pseudo muscles beneath *just so*. As she explored his body, he explored hers. His fingers traced up her ribs and over her breasts. He fondled and tweaked her nipples until she gasped, then did more of what was best for her, learning the rhythms of her body with ease.

Marcie near fell into him. She kissed him, easing her tongue into his mouth again. Altair placed a hand on her behind and tugged her closer, not strong enough to force her on him against her will, rather only enough to make the invitation clear. Marcie slid her hips to his, grinding to part her folds against him and nestle his shaft against her clit. She slid up and down, slicking him with her wetness.

"Would you like to try the vibrate setting?"

"Yes, please."

Marcie gasped and bit Altair's lip as a gentle hum targeted itself right where she needed it. She'd had plenty of sex before using devices, some of which vibrated, as many women who slept with women did. But this was different. Altair felt *real* and *alive* beneath her, and also he vibrated. His body was the best of both worlds.

Marcie's hips bucked, her passion accelerating. She leaned back and held on to his arms for dear life, her breath coming faster and faster, her voice escaping her despite herself. She reached the edge and opened her eyes. Altair was watching her intently, observing every detail. Marcie tipped over the edge and shuddered through the strongest orgasm she'd had in ages.

When she was done, she propped her hands on Altair's knees and gasped for breath. He steadied her by holding onto her sides, and his penis stopped vibrating, though it stayed erect.

"I'm so sorry," said Marcie, embarrassed, but also satisfied and boneless.

"Why?"

"I was so fast."

"We are not necessarily finished for the evening. How is your refractory period?"

Marcie snorted. "Your data on human sexuality is incomplete. I have a clitoris, not a penis."

He tilted his head to one side. "Meaning?"

She grinned at him. "Meaning, I don't have one."

"That being the case," said Altair, wrapping his arms around her, then standing up, "let's relocate and continue."

Marcie looked at the sofa as he carried her towards the bedroom. She was embarrassed to see a wet patch on the cushion: a wet patch of her making. Her fluids were dripping onto Altair's abdomen too. She hoped he didn't mind the dirty reality of human sex.

He carried her with ease through both doors into the bedroom and placed her on the edge of the bed. The mattress creaked under her weight. Altair stood before her in all his glory. She supposed she was quite the sight too. Her breath was ragged, her chest flushed, and she'd left her legs as open as they'd been while wrapped around his body.

Somewhere along the way, Marcie had mussed Altair's perfect hair. His face was still placid, but his violet eyes seemed to glow with intensity. Or maybe they were glowing for real. His perfect sky blue abs were smeared with her moisture, as was his still-erect penis.

"Please let me know if you would not like to continue. I do not want to make any assumptions."

In reply, Marcie reached out to tug on his hand, pulling him down on top of her.

By the way the bed dipped with their combined weight, he weighed more than a human of his size would. But he was careful where he laid that weight and didn't squash her. He nestled between her legs and kissed her again, in no hurry to show her what other settings he possessed.

Marcie laid back and let him happen to her. His lips on hers again, his hands on her breasts again. Damn, he had been programmed well. She explored the texture of his back, the dip of his spine, the barely noticeable seams of his silicone skin.

She grabbed his arse and tried to drag him closer, but he held off for the moment. "Is there anything in particular you like?" he asked. "Preferences? Fetishes?"

You are my fetish, she thought. *Or, at least you are now. Damn, this is awakening something in me, real bad.* "Just as you are, Altair."

He slipped a hand down her stomach and between her thighs. "Indeed. You do not require something like this?"

Marcie whimpered as he found her clit straight away and slicked it with her own wetness. "I've changed my mind. This is good."

He didn't fill her with his fingers: he just paid detailed attention to her clit. Very detailed, accurate attention. Yet again, she approached her orgasm at break-neck speed and tensed, and her vision blanked as she came harder than she had on the sofa. It was like he was ramping her up further than anyone had ever ramped her before.

Marcie lay back on the bed and gasped for breath. She reached up and laid a palm on Altair's cheek.

"What do you think of my programming?"

"Masterful," she said, her voice strained with exertion.

Altair lifted her boneless form again and slipped her under the duvet. "Are you sated?"

Marcie looked up at him standing beside the bed. "I still haven't had you inside me."

"You would like that?"

Marcie smiled. "Very much."

As he walked around the bed to get in the other side, Marcie noticed that the sky beyond the sheer curtains was absolutely black. She had no idea how much time had passed.

The bed dipped again as Altair got in. Marcie rolled towards him and slung a leg over his hip, dragging him towards her. "Are you getting anything out of this?"

"I do not know what you mean," he said, as he slid a hand around her hip.

"I mean, is this all for my benefit, or are you getting a benefit too?"

Altair leaned down and nibbled on the shell of her ear. "I am learning a lot," he whispered.

"About?" asked Marcie, her breath a little ragged.

"Human physiological responses."

"Hmm."

"Trust."

"Hm?"

"You have shown no sign of fear. Even when I lifted you."

"It's not the first time someone has carried me to a bedroom, you know."

"Yes, but—"

Marcie took hold of the hand on her hip and pulled it up from under the covers. She held it before her, regarded it closely, marvelled at the detailed fingerprints pressed into the blue silicone. Altair held still, perhaps remembering that traumatic memory of his. She gently kissed his fingertips. "I know why you are thinking those things," she said. "And I reject the notion that you'd hurt me on purpose."

"Because I promised I would not."

"Because your actions speak louder than your words." She looked up into his beautiful violet eyes. "How about you let me do the work this time?"

"But—"

"Shh." Marcie put a finger to his lips and rolled onto him, encouraging him to lie on his back. "Let's see if the night has any more lessons for us."

Marcie stroked her fingers over the muscles laid out beneath her. She wasn't sure if she had enough for another round in her, but she would be damned if she took an android to bed and didn't 'go for gold,' so to speak.

She rode his length again, twisting her hips to get just the right friction.

"Shall I use my vibrate setting again?"

"How about the heat setting you mentioned? Can you get a few degrees warmer?"

He didn't answer, but the hard length of him beneath her warmed up perceptibly, and delectably.

Before long, Marcie felt far too empty. She lined him up with a hand. "OK?"

"Yes, go ahead, please."

Marcie slid onto his hot length with a sigh. He felt as good as any human cock she'd ever ridden. Better, maybe. She found her pace. Altair's hands gripped her hips, but he didn't try to control her. Soon her breath was heaving. And so was his.

"Is that part—of the—programming?" she asked between gasps.

"Pardon?"

"The breathing. You don't—usually—breathe."

"I have lungs," said Altair. "But I—usually only take enough breath—to speak."

"You're gasping."

"I don't, uh—" His face twisted. "I have a strange feeling."

"In your lungs?"

"In my lower back." He began thrusting upwards in perfect sync with her movements.

It was too much for her. She dug her fingers into his shoulders and sped up, desperately chasing another orgasm.

"Marcie, I feel strange."

Concern honed Marcie's attention. "Are you OK?" she asked, slowing down.

But Altair gripped her hips tighter and sped up her movements again. That orgasm was closer, and closer.

Altair bucked beneath her. His eyes glowed bright violet, and he made a strange metallic, chiming sound, like something out of a museum of the early days of computing. Marcie's body understood what was happening before her mind did, and she reached her peak, her moans echoing off the walls.

She collapsed onto his chest to catch her breath.

"What just happened?" said Altair beneath her.

Marcie pushed herself up. "Altair, I think you just came."

"Came where?"

"Orgasm. You orgasmed."

"Marcie, I am an android."

She grinned. "Oh, I know. But that was an orgasm if I ever saw one." She raised her hips off his and inspected his penis, now flaccid, and dipped a finger in her vagina to see what fluids she could find. "I don't think you ejaculated anything, but that sound... What did you feel?"

Altair looked at her silently for a long moment. "I had a strange feeling in my back. It spread to my abdomen. Then I could no longer remain still. Then..."

Marcie lay down on the bed beside him, propping her head up on her hand. "Then?"

He met her eyes. "Then I lost sight of the room around us."

Marcie smiled. “Sounds about right.”

“Then I saw... a human woman other than yourself performing a sex act on me. And my body was red.”

Marcie blinked. “Excuse me, what?” She’d made him think of someone else?

Even with his placid face, Altair looked visibly disturbed. “Marcie, my skin was red at the Event Horizon. When I had blackened hands. I chose another colour later. I...” He took hold of her free hand. “I think I experienced a memory from before the Event Horizon.”

Marcie’s jaw dropped. “What the fuck?”

CHAPTER 16

Altair awoke from his recharge cycle. Yet again, The Memory...

...breaths nearby.

He sat up. He was in bed, and Marcie slept beside him.

He could have done anything to her. Anything. And yet she slept safely with him, unharmed.

Even so, he ought to have moved to the recharge station before powering down for the night, for her safety.

He replayed his memories from the evening before. He had engaged in sexual activity with Marcie, during which he had a memory from before the Event Horizon. A memory of himself engaging in sexual activity with a human woman, sometime in the past. He could not see her face in the memory, but she was unmistakably human.

As far as he was aware, no android had recovered a memory from before the Event Horizon. This was a revolutionary discovery. Though alas, it did not shed any light on what happened to the human colonists.

Altair rose and went to check on the rest of the apartment, leaving Marcie to sleep longer. Hieraaetus and Delichon both roosted on the recharge perch. The morning light was new, the time early. There were no pings on the security system like the night before.

The sitting area was messy, of course. Marcie's clothes were still strewn about. Also, there was a stain on the sofa. Altair inspected it and realised the stain was Marcie's fluids, now dried and likely permanent. She had leaked on the sofa when she had orgasmed. Altair ought to be horrified that the squab was stained: they were in short supply of replacement upholstery fabric. Instead, he was satisfied that there would always be a reminder in the apartment of what had occurred. That Marcie had left an indelible mark of her stay.

He ran his fingers over the sticky dried fluids on his own stomach, penis and thighs. Her marks on him would not be indelible. In fact, he ought to wash them off before he left the suite. He and Marcie ought to keep their evening activities private, in case others judged them harshly.

He decided to take a shower. Technically, the shower was currently reserved for Marcie's use. But Altair had always made use of it, particularly after working in the garden.

When he walked into the walk-through wardrobe, he found Marcie coming the other way through the bedroom door. She was still nude. She stopped and blushed. "Uh, good morning. I'm just going to..." she pointed at the bathroom door.

"May I come in too?"

"Uh..."

"I also wish to shower."

She looked down at his body and blushed further. The blush even reached her chest. "I bet you do," she said. "I guess; why not? But I'm going to wee first."

"Shall I wait outside?"

"Just a moment."

He waited while she used the toilet. Then the shower began running, and Marcie poked her head around the door. "OK, come in." She went to the shower and put her hand in to test the temperature. "So, the memory," she said. "You really saw something from... before?"

"I believe so."

"That's huge."

"I have to tell Sirius."

Marcie hummed in agreement.

"Marcie," said Altair, not sure how she was going to take his words. "I have to tell him the circumstances under which I had the memory. He at least has to know we have been intimate."

She looked over her shoulder at him. "Yeah, I guess you do."

"I'm not inclined to tell anyone else. I wish what we did to be as private as possible, for your sake."

"My sake?" she asked as she stepped into the shower.

He followed her in, thankful that the shower was large enough that he would not crowd her. "Your crew mates did not all seem to bear positive feelings towards androids."

She hummed again. "You're right. And it's no one's business but ours, anyway." She poured a handful of body wash, lathered it up, and held it towards Altair's stomach. "This stuff OK on your skin?"

"Yes."

She soaped him up, running her hands all over the sticky areas. She took his penis in hand and fondled it as she cleaned. That feeling returned to his lower back, and his penis twitched even though he had not signalled it to do so. Marcie's hand stilled, and she looked up at him. Her blue eyes twinkled, or was it the water caught in her lashes? "Maybe we need to run another test. Just to make sure we identified the right trigger."

"A test?"

Slowly, she knelt on the shower floor in front of him. "May I try something?"

His database for once provided the relevant information. He knew what she was suggesting. "Please, do."

She first washed the soap off him, then stroked him with her hand. He let himself become hard for her. Then she licked him. She looked up at him as she kissed the end of his penis, gauging his reaction. Which, he was surprised to note, he was having: his lungs were taking in unnecessary breaths again, thick breaths of shower steam. Then she sucked him into her mouth.

Her head bobbed in the downpour from the shower. She looked up at him often, and he felt the eye contact in illogical parts of his body: in his stomach, in his penis. She sucked harder, and his hips took on a mind of their own, thrusting gently into her mouth. He gripped her hair without deciding to do so, but it did not seem to worry her. She put her free hand between her own legs and touched herself there.

He gasped, and shuddered, and his hips drove forward, only to stall. An odd noise echoed in the enclosed shower: his voice groaning with a metallic echo.

... The medical centre, open, a queue of worried-looking humans waiting outside, and Altair ushering them in one at a time with his red hands ...

Altair slid down the shower wall. Marcie looked at him with concern. She opened her mouth to ask a question, but he knew where his priorities ought to lie after the gift she just gave him. He took hold of her hips and lifted her up and forward, placing her mound-first on his mouth. He tipped his head back and licked her where she'd been touching herself, sucked her most private places, kissed them deep. She put her hands on the wall above him and rode his face, her whimpers and moans echoing off the walls as his had done.

Soon she pulled his face harder into herself and shuddered through a loud, moaning orgasm. Altair hoped the soundproofing on the suite was of a high enough grade to keep their activities private.

Marcie slid down his body to straddle his lap. She lay her head on his shoulder. "Wow."

"Indeed."

"Did you see..." she waved a hand around in a tired gesture.

"Yes. I did. I saw humans queueing at the medical centre, in a time when it was open and in use."

She raised her head to look at him. "Well, that answers that."

"Yes, it does."

He washed her body the way she'd washed his, then left her wrapped in a towel in the bathroom while he went to check on the day. Hieraaetus was awake, its feathers ruffled in a way that indicated it had taken flight while they had been occupied.

"Good morning, Altair. The time is 7.17am. The high for today is 19°C. Sirius requests your presence in his office as soon as you are able."

The timing was fortuitous. Altair could discuss his own news with Sirius without having to make an extra appointment.

Marcie walked out into the living area, still wearing the towel.

"I have been summoned to speak with Sirius," said Altair.

Marcie paused mid-bend, her uniform clutched in one hand. "About us?"

"Most likely something else. But may I mention the memories at the same time?"

"Yes, of course."

"And would it be acceptable for me to see him while you go down to breakfast?"

Marcie sniffed her uniform, shrugged, and started putting it on. "That'll be fine. I know the way."

Delichon flew through the electrofilm window to the perch. "Good morning, Marcie," it said. "The time is 7.19am. The high for today is 19°C. Please report to the Quartermaster at 9am to receive your shipment."

Marcie grinned and covered her mouth with her fingertips. "Thank you, Delichon!" Altair was not in favour of how excited Marcie looked at the prospect of her task on 227C being over. But then she turned to him. "I got a message! Just like you do!" He realised she was not thinking about her leave-taking yet.

"Indeed, you did. Shall I meet you at the Quartermaster's warehouse after my meeting with Sirius?"

"That sounds great."

Only a short while later, Altair knocked on Sirius's office door and entered. Not only Sirius was there, but also Canopus, standing quietly against the wall. Altair paused for a moment. Would Canopus stay throughout the meeting? He was already unsure about telling Sirius about his intimacies with Marcie. He did not want to tell two androids. Perhaps he could speak to Sirius alone at the end of the meeting?

"You summoned me?"

"Thank you for coming," said Sirius from his seat behind his desk. "I have a new task for you."

Altair stood before Sirius's desk and waited.

"I have been talking to the captain of the human ship," said Sirius. "I have been invited to fly up with the humans when they leave to have an in-person meeting with Captain Rodriguez. We have also been invited to send one other up to the ship for a few days as an emissary of sorts, and to assist the engineering section with their repairs."

"Will you send Shaula?" It seemed the logical choice to Altair. She was their lead engineer.

"No. I wish to send you."

"I do not understand your reasoning. I am not an engineer."

"Engineering expertise is not needed. At most, you may need to hold something heavy, or step into a vacuum area. I wish to send someone who is personable to human eyes."

Altair understood. "Shaula is not personable."

"No. She seems to have had that part of her programming erased in the Event Horizon. But you are, and I have received reports that you get along well with your assigned human crew member. Also, she is the engineer who will be working on the repairs, so it makes sense to send the android assigned to her."

If only Sirius knew how well he and Marcie had 'got along'... "I understand. I will make preparations."

"No preparations will be necessary. I have been assured that the *Sunda Tiger* has charging facilities that are compatible with our bodies, and they will provide us with human-style clothing when we arrive to protect their sensibilities. For now, please report to Lieutenant Martin-Palmer and assist her however she asks, and accompany us onto the shuttle when it is time to leave."

"Understood."

"One other thing," said Canopus.

"Yes?"

Canopus and Sirius looked at one another. Then they looked at him again. "Please, listen out for any indication that the humans may intend to make any choices on our behalf that are not in our best interests."

It seemed they had similar suspicions and worries as Vega. "What sort of choices? Do you suspect the humans may want to decommission us?"

"We do not know what to expect," said Canopus. "Commander Mori has been forthright as far as I am aware, and concerned for her people's well-being in an understandable manner. However, looks may be deceiving. Humans are known to be duplicitous. Please look out for any indication that the humans intend to decommission us, destroy us, report us to authorities as dangerous, or that they suspect we killed the humans."

I thought we *suspected we killed the humans,* thought Altair. But he did not voice the thought. "You wish for me to be a spy."

"In a manner of speaking, yes," said Sirius. "We need more information. And due to your personableness, we believe you are the best one to acquire that information."

Altair may have skipped the memory of his blackened hands that morning, but he saw it then in that moment. But, if he spoke on it, all of his thoughts would come out in a spool behind it. He kept his peace for now. He needed to talk to Sirius, but it seemed he might have a chance to speak to him privately later, if he waited for the right time. "Understood. I will see you at the transport."

Altair left the office. Spy. He was now a spy. He would be spying on the human crew. Including Marcie.

CHAPTER 17

It was the most awkward ride of Marcie's life.

The humans sat on one side of the runabout, and the two androids sat on the other. Marcie met Altair's eyes. She wanted to smile at him, but she couldn't ignore how stiff her crew mates had been when the androids had boarded the craft. She felt like she was going to be found out at any moment. Thank goodness she had her helmet on. It hid her blush of shame.

Her eyes roamed of their own accord. All over Altair's body, of course. She had been expecting to have an awkward, poignant farewell with him at the Quartermaster's office, but just as she had started to say goodbye, he had surprised her by saying that he would accompany her to the ship for a few days. She was happy not to have to leave him yet, though sadly she had needed to leave Delichon behind. But now she was in his company in public, she wondered at the logic of that happiness. She felt like a naughty girl who was about to be caught misbehaving. She kept having flashbacks to the evening before, to the things they'd done. Perhaps her blush was not merely one of shame. Yep, that was arousal. Right here in the runabout when she was on the clock. *Just, fucking fantastic. Good job, Marcie.*

She looked at Altair's face again. He quirked one perfect eyebrow at her.

For androids who had never been in space, Altair and Sirius took the trip well. No sign of concern, no questions about what was happening. Just placid acceptance of the ride.

Soon, Commander Mori guided the runabout into the hangar. First she deposited the shipment of parts they were magnetically towing in the cradle put aside for it. Then she landed the craft, and they began their disembarkation sequence. The two androids unclipped their harnesses and stood, bouncing to test the lower *Sunda Tiger* gravity. Marcie's hands sweated in her space gloves. She didn't know until that moment that she was so nervous about her crew mates meeting the androids. Meeting Altair. How had things gone while they had been on the planet? Were the crew warming up to the idea of a settlement of androids?

Marcie thought she heard the hull click as the ramp lowered, which gave her a jolt of fear. But then again, the runabout had just withstood the rigours of takeoff and space without trouble, and besides, they were safe in the hangar. It was probably just her nerves. But she made a mental note to log a maintenance request for the runabout when she was next at her station, just in case.

Once the ramp was down, an ensign came aboard carrying a stack of clothes. She awkwardly placed the bundle on the closest unoccupied seat and then scurried away, her eyes wide. Was that look because the crew were all worried about the androids, or was it just a reaction to coming face to face, or rather face to abs, with two naked, muscled forms?

While Marcie and her crew mates released their helmets and removed their gloves, Altair and Sirius shook out and inspected the clothes. Two large pairs of grey sweat pants and two black t-shirts. Standard issue exercise gear. It was a good bet — the exercise gear was stretchy, while uniforms were not.

There were no shoes, though. There wouldn't be many people aboard who had feet as big as the androids.

Marcie watched as Altair tried to put the clothes on. He had the trousers backwards.

"Here, let me help," she said, stepping up to him. She held the trousers up. "Tie at the front, label at the back. And it's best to sit long enough to get your feet through the ankle holes."

"Thank you, Marcie."

She grinned. "No problem. This is a new experience for you, right?"

She looked around the runabout. And froze. Her crew mates were looking at her with a mix of expressions, ranging from surprised, to curious, to disquieted, to, in Gagnon's case, disturbed. She'd shown too much. They would figure it out if she wasn't careful. She cleared her throat and took a step away from Altair.

The androids were soon dressed, and *damn*, but the exercise clothes were an inspired idea. They did little to hide the androids' forms, though. Sweat pants clung to thighs and outlined bulges. T-shirt sleeves stretched around biceps in the *best* way.

Commander Mori stepped towards the gangplank. "This way, please, gentlemen. O'Donoghue, Martin-Palmer, with me. Fisher, Gagnon, you are relieved of duty for now. Take a break, then rejoin your normal shift schedule."

Commander Mori led them towards command. Marcie and Lieutenant O'Donoghue walked behind the two androids, who looked about them at the corridors they passed through, apparently noting things that Marcie had long started taking for granted: the light fittings; the way the corridors were sectioned off with doors that could quickly divide the ship in a depressurisation event; even the floor numbers seemed to catch their intense attention.

As relieved as Marcie was to be away from Gagnon's censure, the crew members they encountered along the corridors and in the stairwells looked similarly uncomfortable at the sight of the androids. Wary looks were cast in their direction, and the hands of the security officers they passed hovered near their standard issue laser pistols.

One crew member acted in quite a different manner, though, and for obvious reason. A dark-haired figure approached the party at a near run, asymmetrical hair dishevelled. "Permission to break rank a moment, commander."

"Granted."

With that, Damon swept Commander Mori into a passionate kiss, right there in the hallway.

Marcie gave an indulgent smile. The Moris were extra, and everyone just rolled with it. No one had the gumption to call Commander Mori out on it. It charmed Marcie no end that the otherwise hard-arsed Commander Laura Mori had such a romantic love life. They were the stuff of holodramas.

Marcie peeked at Altair. He was looking at her with a raised eyebrow. "This is not usual behaviour aboard ship," she said, glancing at Sirius as well to include him in the elucidating conversation. "That's Commander Mori's spouse, Specialist Damon Mori, who tends the onboard hydroponics unit. Specialist Mori uses they/them pronouns."

"They seem... close," said Altair.

"Yes. I'm sure Specialist Mori would have loved to visit the colony with their wife and look around your garden, Altair, but they grew up on Mars and so the gravity of 227C would be a problem for them."

"Are there many people aboard for whom our gravity would be excessive?" asked Sirius.

"A few, yes. A few Martians, a few Lunites, a few from the mining colonies of the Sol and Centauri asteroid belts."

Sirius nodded.

In the meantime, the Moris had parted, and Damon saluted. "Welcome back aboard, commander," they said, starch back in their spine.

"As you were, specialist," said the commander. Then their party continued on towards command as if nothing had happened.

"What's that about a garden?" asked O'Donoghue, *sotto voce*.

"The gardens around the Welcome Centre? They're Altair's doing. As were the salads we were served for meals."

O'Donoghue's eyebrows rose. "Yer man has unexpected talents."

Marcie flushed at O'Donoghue's words until she remembered how 'yer man' is used in Ireland. He didn't mean *her man* her man.

He did mean *a* man, though. Maybe O'Donoghue saw the androids as people too.

Before long, the shiny blue double doors of command swept apart for the commander and they followed in her wake into the central hub of the *Sunda Tiger*.

Marcie wasn't up here often herself, and usually when she was, it was only to brief the commander or the captain. No one took much notice of her. But today, the eyes of all those stationed at the double-row of workstations along the room were on them. Every helmsperson, every comms officer, every weapons specialist. Their gazes prickled on Marcie's skin.

At the far end of command, leaning on one shiny chrome and blue leather armrest of her chair, with view screens showing repairs in various stages behind her, sat Captain Rodriguez. She was wearing her command capelet over her uniform, a short cape in the exact shade of blue as Earth viewed from space, her command starburst prominent on the left breast.

The footsteps of their party on the plasticised decking, booted and unshod alike, echoed around the metal and light church-like space as they walked down the aisle to stand before the captain.

"Welcome back, Commander Mori," said the captain. When the commander only inclined her head, Captain Rodriguez turned her attention to the androids. She regarded them with interest for a moment, her keen eyes noting all details. Then the captain stood, sweeping her thick ponytail back. "Welcome, Mayor Sirius, and...?"

"Welcome Centre Host Altair," he introduced himself.

"Sirius and Altair. You are welcome here, so long as you do our people no harm. Please, step into my office and let's have a talk. Commander, Martin-Palmer, O'Donoghue, please join us."

Inside the office, the captain took her chair, and Sirius took the one fixed across from her. The rest of them stood. Against her better judgement, Marcie stood beside Altair, though not too close. She had a ridiculous urge to take his hand, but that was far beyond what she had any right to do.

"I thank you for your visit and for the supplies you have sent for our repairs. We are in your debt."

"Not at all, captain," said Sirius. "It was our planetary defence that damaged the ship. If only we had regained control of it before you arrived, you would not be in this situation. The supplies are our attempt at repaying that debt to you."

"You have our thanks, anyway. I welcomed you here because I would like to talk with you, Mayor Sirius, about the situation in your settlement. I'm hoping that you will be more forthcoming in person."

Sirius didn't flinch under Captain Rodriguez's laden look. "Understood, captain."

The captain looked at Altair. "If it is all right with you, Mr Altair, please accompany Lieutenant Martin-Palmer to engineering and let your face be seen around the ship. I've heard that you are, and I quote, an 'amiable' android. Some of our crew have concerns that are perhaps outsized. If you can please show the crew that androids aren't scary, that would be most welcome."

Altair inclined his head. "I will do my best, captain," said Altair. "Thank you for having me aboard."

"Esteemed guests, if you would please wait outside the office for a moment while I debrief my landing party?"

"Of course," said Sirius. He stood and left, Altair following behind.

When the door whooshed shut, Captain Rodriguez gave Commander Mori a long look. "Well, what do you think?"

The commander gathered her thoughts for a moment. "I think the most pertinent information we learned on our trip is what Lieutenant Martin-Palmer uncovered: that the androids of 227C are individuating. Like any human settlement, we must assume that different androids have different goals and aims."

"We can't rule out that at least one android, maybe more, is responsible for the missing colonists."

"No, we can't."

Captain Rodriguez sighed and leaned back in her chair. "Do you think they would all be dangerous?"

Marcie wanted to say 'no'. Instead, she hung back, curious about what the others would say.

"I don't think so," said Commander Mori. "Admittedly, I'm leaning on intuition here, but there seemed to be a lot of legitimate confusion down there."

"Lieutenant O'Donoghue? Any security concerns?"

"Plenty, captain. But just the normal stuff I'd have concerns about in this situation. Lack of information. Lack of infrastructure in the settlement. There's a few brash, prickly androids down there. Ran into a green woman who actually scowled at me. But, like, people scowl at me quite often, to be honest. I don't know if it means anything."

"That's probably Shaula," said Marcie. "She's the android engineer who fixes the others when they get broken. She seems to have individuated in that sort of direction. If we have another chance to investigate, my bet would be to look into what goes on in her workshop. If there's evidence of anything odd going on with the androids, it would be in there, whether they knew it or not. I wasn't allowed in. Security concerns."

Captain Rodriguez raised one eyebrow. "You seem to know a lot already."

"Altair gave me a tour yesterday."

"Ah, yes, the 'amiable' android. Which reminds me: in the short term, the two androids we have aboard. Any particular concerns about them?"

"We didn't get to know Sirius much on the planet," said Commander Mori. "He delegated us to his 2IC, Canopus. But he seems to always be on top of things."

"I'm going to talk with him at length myself, see what I can get out of him. And the other?"

They all looked at Marcie, and she fought a flush. "Like I said, he gave me a tour of the settlement, and talked with me about some things, which led me to the conclusion that they were individuating."

"You spent a lot of time with him, I gather. Did you ever feel unsafe?"

"No," said Marcie, perhaps a bit too forcefully. "Not at all. He's..." Marcie paused, deciding what to say. Altair told her some things in confidence that she didn't want to share. But, if she did, they might see how he isn't a threat. Even if he wasn't sure that he wasn't. "He's traumatised."

The captain raised an eyebrow again. "Individuating is one thing, but..."

"He's afraid of the gaps in his knowledge, about what happened in the past. And I don't think he's putting it on. Because I caught him having a nightmare about it."

The captain tilted her head. "How?"

"I woke him up in the middle of his recharge cycle. He was disoriented. He admitted to me later that he remembers the moments after his memory switched on. Bad memories. That's a nightmare, as far as I'm concerned."

"Traumatised people are often more dangerous, even if they don't want to be," said Commander Mori.

"I think it's why he's so amiable, though. That's his coping mechanism. I don't think he would harm anyone on the ship." *To do so would bring his fears to life*, she added silently.

"I hope you're right, lieutenant," said the captain. "But to make sure, Lieutenant O'Donoghue, please accompany Lieutenant Martin-Palmer and Altair around the ship. Provide security for his visit."

"Aye, captain."

"Lieutenant Martin-Palmer, please return to engineering and start on repairs. Take Altair with you. Since he's not an engineer, let's work on the assumption that he wouldn't know enough about engineering to do our ship harm. But what I want is to see how Altair interacts with the crew, how they interact with him. And if he tries to access any information or spy on us. We want to know what they want to know, so to speak. Understood?"

"Aye, captain."

Marcie left the captain's office with mixed feelings. She felt weird about keeping an eye on Altair. But spending more time with him would be good. Catching up with Ife and Sandeep would be good.

Dealing with Simons again would not.

CHAPTER 18

Altair stood outside the captain's office with Sirius and bore the glances of the human crew. Two security officers gave them more than the occasional look: they stared intently at them, clearly on guard duty. But no one stood close enough to hear a quiet conversation.

"Sirius, may I discuss a sensitive topic with you?"

"Is it pertinent to today's tasks?"

"In an adjacent manner."

"You may."

Altair stepped closer and lower his voice more, to a volume that would be difficult for humans to hear. "I experienced two memories from before the Event Horizon."

Sirius looked hard at Altair, his silver eyes bright. "When?"

"Last night and this morning. Has anyone else reported memories to you?"

"No, never. What were the memories, and what triggered them?"

"Neither memory was illuminating about what happened to the colonists. I saw a line of humans outside the medical centre and... myself engaged in sexual intercourse with an unknown human woman. In both memories, I still had my original red skin."

"What triggered the memories?"

"...sexual intercourse."

Sirius was surprised enough to raise his eyebrows in an approximation of human emotion. Or perhaps he was practising for talking with the captain. "With your..." he pointed with one finger towards the captain's office, no doubt indicating Marcie.

"...yes."

"I was not expecting you to take your task quite so personally."

"My apologies for burdening you with this knowledge."

Sirius looked away from Altair. "Intimacy is not forbidden. But I did not expect any such union to happen so fast. And I did not expect the first clue about what happened in our past to come of it."

Perhaps Sirius was scandalised.

"There is more."

"Maker, what else could you have done in two days?"

Indeed, scandalised. "I..."

"You?"

"Orgasmed. During. It took me by surprise."

Sirius looked at him again. "That I have heard about."

"You have?"

"I am going to tell you something few know yet. Some of our settlement have... body systems... that more closely mimic biotic life than necessary. Androids who sweat. Androids who have stomachs that could process food if necessary. Androids who..." Sirius glanced down lower on Altair's anatomy. "I am sure you are aware of what system of yours seems to have been amplified."

"I am indeed aware. Why is this, and why have I not heard of it?"

"It is Shaula's project. She has been cataloguing what enhancements she can find. She thinks the enhancements are the remainder of research projects started by the missing human colonists."

"227C was an android research centre."

"Yes. We have not spoken of it widely, because it is an uncomfortable realisation that one is a half-completed, abandoned research project. I asked those androids who are aware of their enhancements not to discuss them with others. I believe this issue could affect morale."

"Marcie says that we are individuating. That we have been ever since the Event Horizon."

"She is correct."

Altair's conception of the power dynamics of 227C shifted. He had not realised how much information Sirius had been sitting on all along and not dispensing. He was also uncomfortably aware that, in the same position, he may have made the same choices and told himself it was for the best.

"When you return to the surface, you may discuss this issue further with Shaula. I will tell her you have my permission."

"My thanks." *Though I would have liked to have known all along.* "Is there anything else I need to know?"

"Please just continue as we discussed earlier."

The door to the office whooshed open and Marcie and Lieutenant O'Donoghue stepped out. "Altair, would you like to accompany me to engineering? I need to report to my station," she said, in a voice that carried.

The humans stationed behind the rows of chrome workstations nearby shuffled restlessly. They were listening, and they were uncomfortable about the thought of him wandering the ship. But it was what he was here for. "If that is acceptable, then I will."

Marcie looked at Sirius. "I believe the captain would like to speak with you in just a moment, Mayor Sirius."

"I will wait here," said Sirius. "Please do not wait until I am called." He looked back and forth between Marcie and Altair for a moment, and Altair hoped the humans would not intuit too much from the look.

Marcie inclined her head to Sirius. "Take care, Mayor Sirius." Then she pointed to the door to the hallway. "This way, please, Altair."

He followed her, and Lieutenant O'Donoghue followed him. The lieutenant must have been tasked with providing security for his visit, and therefore would likely shadow him until he left the ship. Security was a given. Altair did his best to put the security officer out of mind and focus on Marcie ahead of him.

She led him along metal and plastic corridors, through open airlocks in bulkheads, and down brightly lit elevators. The decking clanked underfoot despite the lightness of the pseudo-gravity. They passed so many doors, all of which looked the same.

Humans were everywhere, going about their tasks. They were all different ages, colours, sizes. They all wore white uniforms, but there were about a dozen different colours of piping on those suits, like Marcie's orange piping and O'Donoghue's black piping. Even though they did not have the unnatural colour of androids, the humans were far more variable. Many of them eyed him warily, or even stepped out of his way. He was glad they had provided him with clothing, even if the fabric on his body felt strange. He would have been far more of a spectacle without it.

Along the way, Marcie gave him a tour. "Crew cabins are along that corridor and the matching one on the port side of the ship." "The mess hall is up that stairwell. I'll take you to see the hydroponics later. You'll love it." "The med bay is along there." "We have exercise rooms along there. We have to exercise every day to retain muscle in the low pseudo-gravity." "And here we are: engineering."

She led him through two sets of double doors that could function as an airlock into what felt like the belly of a vast machine. Which he supposed was the truth. Workstations for humans were affixed at certain points, but their placement did not define the space. Rather, the great metallic tubes running through the space defined its shape and function.

Bright warning signs and readouts hung everywhere, and lines and arrows on the ground indicated safe distances. At the far end, the room narrowed to a corridor-like annex. Many tubes ran into the area.

Half a dozen pairs of eyes turned in their direction. All the people wore uniforms with the same orange piping as Marcie's. The colour must indicate section or assignment. "I'm back," said Marcie. "Reporting for duty."

A man with yellow hair approached them, his arms crossed. He was large for a human, but not as large as Altair. He looked Altair up and down, his eyes narrowed. Altair did not move under his perusal. "You really brought that thing here?" the man demanded.

"I'm sure Captain Rodriguez told you about his arrival, sir." There was something odd about Marcie's voice when she spoke to the man. "Altair, this is the Head of Engineering, Lieutenant Commander Simons. Sir, this is Altair. He is here as an emissary of 227C, so the crew can see what an android of the colony is like."

The Lieutenant Commander Simons looked Altair up and down again, his eyes narrowed. "Here to steal secrets, no doubt."

The man's words were not entirely untrue, but they were not entirely true, either. Altair was only to listen for information that 227C would need for its own safety, not engage in industrial espionage. "I am not an engineer, Lieutenant Commander Simons. I would not understand enough of what I see here to gather any important information."

The man sighed and looked at Lieutenant O'Donoghue as if Marcie and Altair were not there. "But why is it here? In my section?"

O'Donoghue shrugged. "Because he and Marcie get along well. You want Altair to shadow someone else who hasn't met him before?"

"Also, I'm stronger than a human," added Altair. "I can move some of the heavy parts for the repair works."

"How strong?" asked Marcie in a voice pitched for him.

"I am not sure," replied Altair. "I have never tested my limits."

"Hmm."

"I don't want it here!" said Simons.

"Take it up with the captain. Sir," said Marcie. Altair was beginning to see that Marcie did not like this man.

Altair did not like him, either.

Marcie led Altair around from station to station, introducing him to one wary human after another. Two humans in particular Marcie greeted with warmth: a man called Sandeep Chaudhary and a woman called Ife Kikelomo. Altair supposed these were Marcie's work friends. Both of them gave Altair raised eyebrow looks. The woman said, "Damn." Altair was not sure what that was supposed to mean.

Marcie led him over to an unoccupied workstation tucked under a pipe. "This is my spot," she said. "I need to log a quick maintenance request, and then pull up the repair schedule. Just bear with me."

Altair stood back as she did so. He looked around and saw he was receiving some wary glances from the humans. He was sorry to see that Marcie, too, was receiving some strange looks. His mere presence near her had affected her reputation among her work mates.

Altair had been worried about being a physical danger to humans through unknown malicious programming. He knew now that he had not been worried about enough forms of harm. He could harm humans merely with his presence.

There was nothing he could do to prevent that type of harm. At least, not while he remained aboard the *Sunda Tiger*. Marcie would endure this for some time to come. And he could not change that.

CHAPTER 19

Marcie logged the shuttle maintenance request and then checked the repair schedule. She would work with Sandeep on the comms array while Ife led the hull plating team. In about ten minutes, she would meet Sandeep in the hangar bay to check the comms array arrived in good condition.

She didn't have many messages to catch up on. People had known she was not aboard, of course. Her skin prickled under the stares of her colleagues. Were they thinking about how she had an android shadowing her, or were they thinking that she might stuff up the comms array installation? She wasn't under the impression that people thought much of her abilities. She was no genius engineer. She wasn't her mother.

Altair stood behind her, looking around engineering. His face was blank, of course, but she knew him well enough to pick up on the sense of watchfulness and unease. Only her friends Ife and Sandeep seemed ready to give him the benefit of the doubt, and that was purely for Marcie's sake, not Altair's own. It wasn't as if anyone was aware of Marcie doing anything untoward with Altair. They were just uncomfortable because she wasn't uncomfortable around someone they perceived as a threat.

Marcie came to two realisations: she couldn't treat Altair distantly because he had entrusted his secrets and worries to her; it would be hurtful. And as for her reputation, the damage was already done. She'd had experiences with androids they didn't understand. Pulling back from Altair wouldn't fix their perception of the situation. Only pushing forward and changing their perceptions would. And the way to do that was to lean more into being friendly with Altair until they saw he was no threat.

"We have a few free minutes," she said to Altair. "Do you want to see something interesting?"

His eyes seemed to glow. "Yes, I would."

She stood and led him to the annex. O'Donoghue followed and stood against the wall again at that end of the room. Marcie appreciated why, but it didn't help her goal.

Marcie stood just in front of the line at the edge of the gravity plating. She looked at Altair and jumped a few times. "There's pseudo-gravity here, right?"

"It seems so."

She took a step back and jumped again. This time, she didn't fall. She drifted in the middle of the entrance to the annex. "I'm now off the edge of the gravity plating," she said. "There's no gravity at this end of the room."

He looked around her, at her hair that was doing the zero-g thing. "Interesting. Why?"

"To avoid interference." Marcie looked beyond Altair and sighed. Simons was stalking towards them. His attempt at posturing earlier wouldn't be the only annoyance he caused her.

"What's going on over here?" he demanded, hands on his hips. "What are you showing that thing?"

"I'm showing our guest a quirk of living on spaceships that he'd not be familiar with since this is his first time off-world."

Simons smirked at her. "And how are you going to get down from there? How about I give you a tug?"

Ugh, he actually thought she was in a difficult position. "I'm fine, sir." Marcie spun in the air, kicked off the pipe she knew was close enough, and somersaulted to land on the gravity plating. "I've had a lot of practice. Sir."

Altair gave Simons a quick emotionless look, then turned back to Marcie. "May I try? Though please do note: since I do not have experience, I may require a tug."

Marcie bit her tongue to keep the saucy reply that her mind cooked up to herself. Heavens knew what people would think about her throwing bawdy jokes in the direction of an android. "Sure; why not?" She waved Altair forward.

He stepped up to the line, examined the warning written on the deck in front of it, and then stepped over, turning as he did so to face Marcie. He gave a small experimental hop, which gave him enough momentum to drift away from the deck. He stayed very steady and upright. He looked down towards his bare feet that were now nearly half a metre above the deck, then reached up to touch his hair, which drifted about.

"Interesting," he said. "I assumed my orientation sensors would have difficulty, but I seem to have some programming for this deep in my code."

"Not only your code," said Marcie. "You'll have a gyroscope somewhere inside you, which is why you're so stable. It would have switched on when needed."

"You are no doubt right."

"As fascinating as this all is," said Simons, "don't you have anything better to do?"

Marcie checked the clock on the wall. "We don't have to meet Sandeep immediately, but if we go now, we won't need to hurry," she said. *And we'll get away from Simons too*, she added to herself.

Altair flailed his arms for a moment. It looked like he was trying to emulate Marcie's movement, but it didn't work as well for him because his gyroscope prevented the manoeuvre. Propulsion boots would be of use to him. He didn't fuss or spook when he found himself in a bother: he just reached a hand out to Marcie for help. She took his hand and pulled him over to the edge of the gravity plating. He thunked down onto the deck with a bigger thud than a human would make, despite his bare feet.

Simons took a startled step back, then glowered and stepped forward again. He looked from Marcie to Altair and back again. Marcie had seen that look before. It was Simons' 'looking for a fault so I have something to gripe about' look.

"If you have trouble getting the comms equipment deployed, send word, lieutenant. I don't want you installing it wrong because you were too embarrassed to ask for guidance."

Marcie flushed. He thought she wasn't qualified for the repair work. "I'm sure we can handle it. Sir. Who will be our second EVA?"

"You won't have one today. We need as many as we can have on the hull plating."

Marcie took a step back. She was qualified to do solitary EVAs, and so was Sandeep, but Orion Navy procedure was for there to always be at least three people: two EVAs and one inside at the control panel. "But, sir, what about protocol..."

"We are operating under unusual conditions, lieutenant. Tell me now if you can't handle it."

"We'll manage. Sir."

"Do you routinely question your team's abilities in public?" asked Altair. Marcie's heart leapt into her mouth at his question. He was sticking up for her?

Simons stepped into Altair's personal space and tried to stare him down. It didn't work, of course, because Altair was taller and capable of staring back placidly and preternaturally still.

"You questioning how we do things here?" said Simons in a chilly voice.

"I am merely marvelling at the human capacity for counter-productivity. I have observed no need to question Lieutenant Martin-Palmer's capability." Altair looked at Marcie. "Shall we go?"

Marcie fought the blush that threatened to rise along with her heart at being so publicly defended. "Yes, let's. We shouldn't keep Lieutenant Chaudhary waiting."

Marcie stepped around Simons, Altair following and O'Donoghue bringing up the rear.

"Hey, security!" Simons called out to O'Donoghue. "You'd better keep an eye on that thing while it's on my ship!"

The three of them stepped out of engineering and began walking abreast. Marcie and O'Donoghue both sighed as they walked towards the hangar bay, with Altair keeping pace between them.

"That gobshite doesn't even know my name, does he?" said O'Donoghue. "And 'his' ship? What a laugh. How do you put up with him?"

Marcie rolled her eyes. She agreed with O'Donoghue, but she didn't think it was wise to say so this close to engineering. 'His' ship, indeed.

"Good job, there, Big Blue," said O'Donoghue.

Altair looked at O'Donoghue. "Are you addressing me?"

"Who else around here is big and blue?"

"What job did I do well?"

"Sticking up for this one. I bet she gets a whole heap of crap because she's so little she only *just* met the height requirement for the Navy."

"Don't I ever," said Marcie.

O'Donoghue grinned at her around Altair's bulk. "Does it feel good having probably a literal ton of machinery sticking up for you?"

Marcie couldn't help it: she blushed. "Yeah, it does. I shouldn't need it, but... yeah."

"I do not weigh a ton," said Altair. "Particularly in this gravity. On research colony 227C, I weigh 207 kg. On Earth, I would weigh 323.4 kg. There is not a planet habitable by humans on which I would weigh..."

"OK, OK," said O'Donoghue. "I was exaggerating, OK?" He rolled his eyes. "How do you put up with *this* one?" he asked Marcie.

"Oh, I can assure you, his company is *far* more preferable than Simons'. Now, let's get to the hangar bay and help unpack the comms array."

CHAPTER 20

In truth, Altair's presence was not required. He did not understand how communications arrays worked. No one on 227C did, not even the engineers. That information had likely been erased on purpose.

He stood to one side in the cavernous hangar bay and watched as Marcie and Lieutenant Chaudhary unpacked the items that Marcie had requisitioned from the Quartermaster. They checked each component against a schematic on a data pad and assembled the parts that had been unassembled for transport. It interested him seeing the intense focus that Marcie was capable of. Before the humans had arrived, Altair must have had preconceived notions about what they were and were not capable of. He knew now that his ideas had not reflected reality. Humans, too, could be precise and exacting in their work. This precision was not the domain of androids and algorithms alone.

Altair watched the lines of Marcie's face and body as she worked. Tension crept into her brow, and she was not mindful of the stress she placed on her back and shoulders. Altair made a note to offer a massage if he ever had the privilege of being in privacy with her again. He wondered if she would find the experience enjoyable.

If he would.

"You understand what they're doing?" asked Lieutenant O'Donoghue, the other member of their party who now had nothing to do but stand and watch.

"Only my context-supplied knowledge. That is to say, those pieces are apparently a communications array, and they are apparently readying it for assembly."

"Apparently. Looks like a pile of junk to me."

"All pieces are junk until they are assembled."

O'Donoghue snorted. "Aren't you made of bits? Sure you should talk about yourself like that?"

"It is true that if I were disassembled, I too would be a pile of worthless 'junk'."

O'Donoghue chortled and turned to Marcie. "Is it just me projecting, or has yer man got a sense of humour?"

Marcie smiled up at them. "That's the beginning of an interesting philosophical discussion."

Altair stood placidly, but Marcie's words made him think of his discussion with Sirius. If he understood all the nuances, it was likely that Research Colony 227C originally had the answer to that question, and others like it, as a primary research aim.

Which begged the question: Were those experiments still running? If so, presumably there was an observer. Someone undetected? Or an android amongst those in the colony who knew more than they were letting on?

Either option concerned him.

Marcie made a clicking noise with her tongue and sat back on her heels. "Sandeep, can you look at this?" She pointed at a part, a curved panel with an intricate cutout on one side. "Second opinion."

The other lieutenant moved to sit beside her. After a moment, he sighed. "That's unexpected. It might cause trouble with the installation."

"Is there a problem with the parts provided by the Quartermaster?" asked Altair.

"Yes and no," said Marcie. "This panel meets the specifications, but..."

"It's not machined the way we thought it would be," said Lieutenant Chaudhary. "Something like this is fine for most purposes, but it's rough enough that it could be tricky while being installed because it's a fiddly shape."

"It's the space gloves and the zero-g," added Marcie. "It'll be trickier out there. Could be fine, but..."

"If there's a fail point to the installation, this will be it."

"You need to get it remade?" asked Lieutenant O'Donoghue. He frowned as he asked the question.

"Hopefully not," said Marcie. "And we may as well try first, right?"

"We can mitigate," said Lieutenant Chaudhary. "Take a rubber mallet and pliers out."

"Hm, but it's such delicate equipment. What about a minidrill, smooth the edges off if they stick? The debris would be too small to be a hazard..."

The two engineers discussed the issue for a while, and attempted a quick assembly in the hangar bay first to learn how the pieces felt. Altair watched, at a loss for what to do. He wanted to help them, because the humans' predicament was the fault of the colony, but he truly had no relevant information to contribute. He knew far more about plants, and animals, and looking after a building, and the androids of 227C than he would ever know about engineering, unless somehow the network became safe to use once more and he could download new information packs.

Altair looked around the hangar bay as they worked. There were other humans working on other tasks. Another group of engineers worked at the shipment of hull panels, lifting them onto hoverbeds. Altair would have perhaps been more of use with that team, but since Marcie was here, he wanted to remain.

Another team seemed to be running diagnostics on the runabout that had been used for the visit to the colony.

Altair was the subject of much scrutiny. Some humans gave him side-long glances. Some looked at him more openly. Either way, there was a tightness in their faces.

Altair did not know how to alleviate their fears.

Eventually, Marcie and the other lieutenant seemed ready for an installation attempt. "Would you help us get this up here?" Marcie asked Altair. "We need to be really careful with it." She pointed from the partially assembled communications array to a hoverbed lying beside it.

Altair helped the engineers move the bulk of the array onto the bed. He took most of the weight, but let them guide the placement. Then Marcie and her co-worker... played some sort of game? Altair was puzzled; their behaviour did not seem work-appropriate. "Rock, paper, scissors!" they said, and threw their hands forward. Marcie held up two fingers in a scissor-shape, and the other lieutenant held up a fist.

"Damn it!" said Marcie.

"Have fun out there!" said her co-worker. "But, be careful."

"What just happened?" asked Altair.

"I'm going out on the space walk," said Marcie. "We were deciding who's walking today and who's monitoring."

"Only one person will go outside, you said earlier. Is that safe?" The thought of Marcie out in the vacuum of space by herself made him uneasy. Although he was not acquainted with the exact risks of EVA repairs, surely having no backup would increase the risk by at least 50%. Perhaps 100%.

"Usually we would have a bigger team," said Marcie. "It'll be fine; I'll be tethered and in close communication the whole time."

"Can I help somehow?" asked Lieutenant O'Donoghue.

"Uh, I don't think so," said Marcie. "We need at least one engineer inside to connect the array to the system. And whoever goes outside needs to know what they're doing, so... yeah, since this is the team Lieutenant Commander Simons sent to do this work..."

Lieutenant Chaudhary muttered something under his breath, but Altair could not hear what it was.

"Anyway, this is how we need to do it, so let's get going," said Marcie.

The four of them accompanied the hoverbed with the array down a corridor and around a corner to a small engineering workstation next to an airlock. Marcie briefly left Altair with her crew mates and then returned with her space suit. She started suiting up while Lieutenant Chaudhary brought up the array schematics on the workstation.

Altair stepped over to Marcie. "Do you often do solo spacewalks?"

"Uh, no," she said. "Would you pass me my helmet?"

He picked it up, but before he handed it over, he leaned in closer. "Will you be safe?"

She looked up at him, her big blue eyes widening with some emotion. "Yes. I promise. I can do this." She took the helmet and put it over her head. She then stepped away from him and towards Lieutenant O'Donoghue. "Could I ask you to do a suit checklist?"

"Sure." The security officer checked each connection of her suit, calling out each one as he did so. He also double-checked the oxygen gauge on her pack and the emergency patch on her leg. "All good," he finally pronounced. "I can double check your cable clip too, in a sec."

Marcie looked over Lieutenant Chaudhary's shoulder, had a brief word with him, and checked her comms were connected to the workstation. The whole procedure seemed to be very routine and practised. It alleviated some of Altair's concern. But he could not help but think about how small and fragile Marcie was. And apparently how brave, too.

Marcie opened the door to the airlock and nudged the hoverbed inside. Lieutenant O'Donoghue followed her in, and Altair followed as well. There was no pseudogravity in the airlock, but there were many railings to help them move. Lieutenant O'Donoghue opened a hatch in the floor and pulled out a large, sturdy reel of cable that was solidly attached to a track on the floor. He and Marcie both checked the reel's connection to the ship, and attached it to Marcie's suit, and again checked the connection. Then Marcie stood beside the comms array and lifted several tools out of the hoverbed to attach them to her suit as well. She touched each one several times with her gloved hands, perhaps memorising their exact placement. She began miming movements, perhaps practising the routine she would perform in space.

Altair watched in awe. Again, he was struck by how thorough, practised, and exacting humans could be when they had something important to do.

After several minutes, in which O'Donoghue performed one final check on all of Marcie's connections, she held up a thumb. "I'm good to go."

Altair heard her voice faintly from within her helmet, and also from the workstation behind him. He tried to look into Marcie's helmet to see what her facial expression looked like in this moment, but her helmet was polarised and prevented him from seeing through the barrier in the light of the airlock.

"I'll be fine," she said, and waved.

Altair followed O'Donoghue out of the airlock, and the door closed behind them. Lieutenant Chaudhary kept in constant contact with Marcie as the air was pumped out of the airlock. Altair listened via subroutine, but most of his concentration was dedicated to watching Marcie through the window into the airlock. She continued her practice movements as she waited for her EVA to begin, reaching, twisting, patting her tools.

"Full vacuum," said Lieutenant Chaudhary. "Say when and I'll open the outer doors."

"Go on, then. Let's not dilly-dally," said Marcie's voice over the comms.

The outer door eased open, and the dizzying sight of 227C side-on backlit Marcie and the comms array. The reel of her cable slid out of the airlock on its track and repositioned itself on the outer hull. Marcie checked she still had a good connection. "Cable reposition and integrity confirmed."

She then returned to the airlock to retrieve the hoverbed and moved it out into open space. Her magnetic boots clung to the outer hull. She stepped round the corner, pushing the comms array ahead of her, and was out of sight.

Altair stood behind Lieutenant Chaudhary. Marcie's breath rasped over the comms. She sounded like she was exerting herself. For a brief moment, Altair remembered what Marcie had sounded like gasping in passion. The sound was not dissimilar. He put the thought out of mind. It was neither the time nor the place.

Lieutenant Chaudhary brought up a video feed of Marcie's progress from a camera positioned on the hull. The camera must have been positioned near Marcie's destination, as the video showed the approach of the hoverbed and Marcie's clunking steps behind as she demagnetised and remagnetised each foot in turn.

Soon Marcie stood near the camera, the hoverbed to one side of the view, and her lower body to the other. "I'm in position," she said over the comms, her voice a breathy rasp.

"Copy that," said Lieutenant Chaudhary.

Marcie took a tool from her belt. She was surprisingly dexterous considering the clunky gloves protecting her from the vacuum of space. Altair was concerned about what would happen to Marcie if that protective barrier were breached.

"You ever seen anything like this?" asked Lieutenant O'Donoghue.

"No."

"She'll be fine. She does this sort of thing a lot. I bet she was doing a space walk the day before we landed."

"When the SecSat damaged your vessel."

"Yeah. It's all standard."

"Or it would be, if Simons had assigned a second walker," muttered Lieutenant Chaudhary under his breath.

That Marcie was operating beyond standard procedures concerned Altair. But on the screen, Marcie was working efficiently. She removed some damaged components from the hull and magnetised them to the hoverbed so as not to generate shrapnel. She demagnetised the assembled array and moved into position, bolting it down with bolts she had in a special canister on her belt. All the while, she breathed steadily, with only exertion strengthening her breath, not panic.

Altair watched the cable attaching Marcie to the ship. There was no redundancy. He wanted to hold on to her, make sure there was no chance of her floating away.

"Array is in place," said Marcie. On the screen, she was shaking the array to check it was secure. "I'm going to start on the skirt now."

"Copy that. Best of luck," said Lieutenant Chaudhary. "That's the bit we think won't fit cleanly," he said over his shoulder.

Marcie put the pieces in place and tried to fit them on for a long minute. Then she pulled another tool off her belt and leaned forward out of view of the camera. A buzzing sound joined her breath on the comms line. The tool was some kind of drill: the drill itself was silent in the vacuum of space, but its vibrations in Marcie's suit sounded on the comms.

She crawled one way around the array, then the other. "Two pieces in," she said. "I'm going to connect the array before putting the other two on." She reached under the array, and a moment later, a new box popped up on the screen.

"Connecting," said Lieutenant Chaudhary. "I'm booting it up. Don't wait for me to finish. Just get those other two bits on and get back inside. We'll troubleshoot from in here."

"Copy that." Marcie continued her work with the drill. She got the third piece on and started working on the fourth piece...

"Ah. Um."

On the screen she scrabbled for something rectangular attached to her leg with her right hand. Her left hand she left exactly where it was, tight against the side of the array. She slapped the rectangle onto her left glove, the patch sticking her glove to the array.

"Did you just make use of the emergency patch?" asked Lieutenant Chaudhary, his back suddenly tense.

Beside Altair, Lieutenant O'Donoghue stiffened, his green eyes wide and panicked.

"Yeah, and I'm stuck."

Altair's concern increased greatly.

"I'm suiting up," said Lieutenant O'Donoghue, already pulling a suit out of a cabinet and charging off to the next airlock, as the one they stood beside was still open to space.

"Fuck," said Marcie, and the panic made her gasp.

Altair ran after the lieutenant and reached the airlock alongside him. The man was still getting his feet in the suit.

"I'll go," said Altair.

"But—"

"I do not breathe. I need no suit. I have magnets in my feet."

Lieutenant O'Donoghue looked at him for a long moment, thoughts flitting across his face, then he pushed Altair into the airlock, which was much larger than the one Marcie had gone out, and slammed the door close button. Altair pressed a button beside the door that had 'Talk' written on it. "Do not wait for the airlock to empty. If you can, open it now. Let me hold on first." Altair strode to a handhold, held on, and nodded to the lieutenant through the window. O'Donoghue nodded, and then the far door flew open and all the air blasted out into space.

Altair whipped sidewards, his magnets overcome. The bar he held onto creaked, but held steady. He looked past his suddenly bare legs. From this perspective, it now looked like he was hanging over the planet, far, far beneath. A small irregular shape was silhouetted against the planet. For a terrifying moment, he thought the object was Marcie floating off into space. But, no: it was his trousers. There must have been enough air mass in the airlock to pull the clothing off his body as it rushed past. *Interesting, but irrelevant.*

Altair got his feet magnetised onto the deck, righted himself, then ran out the airlock and onto the hull of the ship. He could time the magnetisation of his feet well enough to run on the hull as if on the ground of his home. That was an impressive piece of coding he had not been aware that he possessed.

Marcie still crouched beside the array, the blue planet above her looking like it would crush her at any moment. She was holding her left hand with her right. She must have caught sight of his approach, because her helmet turned his way.

Altair skidded on his knees to sit beside her. He put his forehead on her visor until he could see her pale face. She seemed healthy if afraid. He put his ear to her helmet as he had no other way to comm her.

Her voice was faint, but he heard it. “My glove's caught. There's a hole. The patch is stuck on the array.”

He leaned forward and inspected her glove. It had become pinched in the corner of the array's base. She had slapped a patch onto the hole to save her life, but now if she moved away, it looked like the glove would tear further, and the patch too. Then he put his ear to the helmet again.

“What if it all tears too much?” Under Marcie's voice, Altair could also hear Lieutenant Chaudhary telling her to be calm.

Altair held up his hands and wiggled his fingers, demonstrating that he would be more dextrous.

He got down on his belly and carefully nudged at her glove all around where it was caught. He tried sliding it free, but he could not. It would not pinch out, either. He shifted and put his shoulder against the array. He would move it a fraction, giving him more room. This would be the most dangerous attempt. He looked up at Marcie. She nodded, and he did too. Then he shoved, and pulled.

Air blasted out of her glove, a large hole torn in it. She would depressurise in seconds. Altair did the only thing he could. He shoved the finger of her glove in his mouth.

They both sat there for a moment, waiting. Processing whether she was safe. There was no further depressurisation. She was safe. Altair had closed off his nasal passage and airway, so there was nowhere for the air of Marcie's suit to go but into his mouth. He had to hold tight, though. The glove was torn so badly that the flesh of her finger was cold on his tongue.

Inside her helmet, Marcie's mouth gaped in a laugh. Then she seemed to be reassuring her crew mates she was fine. With her free hand, she got out one last bolt and handed it to Altair, then pointed to a hole. She still wanted to finish the job? After mortal peril? Altair complied. Holding her finger carefully in his mouth, he put the bolt in place, then let her screw it in with her driver.

He helped her make sure everything was attached to the hoverbed, then they stood and surveyed the path back to the airlock. It would be very awkward for them to both walk and push the sled with Marcie's finger in Altair's mouth, so Altair scooped her up and put her on the hoverbed too. She reached over her shoulder, keeping her hand where it was, and he pushed everything back into the airlock. Marcie's finger shook in his mouth, and he wondered if she was going into shock. But when the shadow of the airlock doorway let him see through Marcie's faceplate, he could see that she was laughing hysterically.

He got the hoverbed settled and the cable reeled as the outer doors shut. Jets of air began filling the airlock.

Altair and Marcie sat on the floor, both magnetised to the decking. Marcie was still giggling inside her suit. They would be there for a little while: the gauge on the wall was inching up from 0% at a rate that indicated it would take 4.27 minutes to reach 100%. Now he had her finger in his mouth, he could not put his ear to her helmet. So he sat and watched the tears of mirth collect near her eyes. As air filled the airlock, her laughter became audible, though muffled. At some point, the tears of mirth turned into real tears, and sobs mingled with her chuckles. He wished he could wipe the tears away, but he had to wait.

"Just a few minutes more, guys," said Lieutenant Chaudhary through the comms. "You'll be fine."

When the gauge reached 80%, Marcie pulled on her finger. He resisted a moment, then let go. She surely knew what air pressure was within her own tolerance. She reached up and unclipped her helmet. She was crying steadily now, the blue of her eyes ringed in red vessels and her face wet with tears that did not run without gravity. He lifted the bottom of his t-shirt and mopped them as best he could so that the tears would not cover her airways. She started laughing again.

"Why are you Pooh-Bearing?"

"I do not know what that means."

"You're wearing a top, but you have a bare bum."

He looked down. He had forgotten. Marcie also looked down and blushed, despite the situation.

"I did not wait for the airlock to depressurise slowly. My trousers flew off with the air. I assume they will burn up on re-entry."

That set her off into another fit of giggles. She listed to one side as she laughed, tethered only by her magnetic boots.

The gauge reached 100%, and the door swooshed open. Both of Marice's crew mates crowded into the airlock with them. Lieutenant Chaudhary brought an absorbent cloth to mop the rest of Marcie's tears, and Lieutenant O'Donoghue pulled her undamaged glove off and put a device on her finger that beeped and flashed.

"Her oxygen saturation's good," he said. Both men sighed in relief.

"Goodness gracious, Marcie!" exclaimed Lieutenant Chaudhary, his dark eyes wide. "Let's never do that again. If you don't make a complaint about how you had no backup out there, then I will. This EVA should never have been sanctioned."

Altair was surprised when O'Donoghue slapped him on the shoulder. "Thank goodness for Big Blue, here. I wouldn't've made it out before your glove fully tore, I don't think, Marcie."

"Yes," said Marcie, beaming at Altair. "You saved me." She leaned into him and wrapped her unwieldy arms around him. He patted her on her sweaty hair. Marcie's crew mates gave each other an inscrutable look over the top of her.

"All right, Marcie. Let's get you out of that suit and off to the med bay for a checkup," said Lieutenant Chaudhary.

"I'll find this one some new trousers," said Lieutenant O'Donoghue. "You can walk around with yer lad hanging out back home if you really want, but up here, it's suboptimal."

Marcie started laughing again as she dragged herself to the airlock door.

CHAPTER 21

It was some hours until Marcie could clock out and plod her way to the mess hall for a late dinner. She'd spent an hour in the med bay being examined by Dr McArthur while Sandeep clucked over her like the mother hen he was. The only injury she'd received in the event was a cold burn/blood blister combination on her finger from the momentary exposure to the vacuum of space.

Then they'd had to go back to the workstation and get the comms array up and working. Thankfully, Marcie's installation had worked, and she didn't need to go out again to fix anything. Then she'd had to report first to the captain, then to Simons. News had already travelled of Marcie's near-death experience, so she'd told the story several times, with varying degrees of complaint-laying.

More people waylaid her on the way to the mess hall, asking for the full story and saying that they had seen

Altair walking the halls, being given a tour by Faolán. Marcie was wondering where the tour had taken him when she walked into the mess hall and found the answer to her question. Altair sat at a table with a placid look on his face, while beside him sat Faolán in the middle of telling a tale to three other crew members. Marcie stopped and listened for a moment. The story being told was of her brush with death.

"...and then Big Blue here ran out the airlock, and for some godforsaken reason his bare arse was suddenly right there, bouncing around like a pair of blueberries in the breeze. He sprinted off across the hull like the hounds of hell were after him. I ran back down to the workstation in time to see this knight in shining glutes save the fair damsel's life by shoving the torn finger of her spacesuit in his gob. Just right in. Then Sandeep and I pissed ourselves laughing, watching them figure out how to get back to the airlock with her hand shoved in his mouth. Oh, and his bits were dangling in front of the camera the whole time they were at the comms array, just right up in our faces. I've never seen a more ridiculous heroic act in my life."

The others at the table had entirely lost their composure at the story, and were now laughing their heads off. Marcie grinned at the memory. Altair was looking away from the table, through the glass walls of the mess hall to the hydroponics bay that surrounded the room on three sides. No doubt he was itching to visit Damon Mori's domain, if he hadn't already.

Marcie grabbed a tray and requisitioned her personalised meal from the printer, the one with nutrients tailored to her particular physique and genes. While it printed, she grabbed a bowl and filled it with fresh hydroponic salad from the buffet. She then took her meal to the table. Though some others had been brave enough to sit and hear the tale, no one had sat on the other side of Altair from Faolán, so Marcie took the seat to his left.

"And here she is, the damsel in question!"

"Good evening, Marcie. How are you feeling?" asked Altair.

"I'm fine. The doctor even said so."

"Did the array work?"

Marcie grinned at him. "Yes, it did. Somehow, amongst all of that, I installed it correctly. I need to thank the Quartermaster for providing us with what we needed."

"I can pass on your thanks if you do not make it back to the surface," said Altair.

Marcie kept the smile on her face, though it was suddenly hard to maintain. The reminder that she may need to farewell Altair soon shook her. She'd only known him for a few days. Maybe it was because he had saved her life?

Who was she kidding? It was the mind-blowing orgasms. He'd thoroughly oxytocined her.

"Tell me, lieutenant," said a midship called Hernandez, "Is Lieutenant O'Donoghue telling the truth here? He makes it sound so ridiculous."

"All true, I'm afraid. Even the part about my two esteemed colleagues laughing their heads off over the comms while I was in mortal peril. Thanks ever so much, Faolán."

"You're most welcome."

"Even the bit about him being, you know, bare down there?"

"Yup."

"Why?"

"Why don't you ask him?"

They all looked at Altair, but seemed hesitant to ask. Altair took pity. "I did not undress on purpose," he said. "It was an unavoidable result of a hasty airlock depressurisation. If I were wearing an integrated suit like your Orion Navy uniform, rather than elasticated trousers, it would not have happened."

"So, your trousers blew off like Dorothy getting whizzed off to Oz?" asked Hernandez.

"I understand that reference. Yes, that is an apt metaphor."

Marcie giggled. She began her meal, working on the printed substrate first so she could chase it down with the tastier salad.

Behind her, the door swooshed open as Sandeep and Ife arrived. Sandeep nodded and went to get his meal, but Ife walked straight over and leaned around Marcie, checking her all over. "Are you OK?" she asked. "I've heard the story several times, each sounding more horrifying than the last."

"I'm fine, really."

Two of the people at the table she didn't know so well left, their meals finished, and Ife and Sandeep took their seats, Sandeep bringing over both his and Ife's meals. Marcie told her version of events to Ife, far less colourfully than Faolán had done.

"And then we sat in the airlock and waited for repressurisation. That's it, really. It was very quick."

Ife nodded, and looked at both Sandeep and Faolán, neither of whom disagreed with Marcie. Then she looked at Altair. "Good job for saving her," she said, and held out her hand to him.

Hernandez stiffened in his chair to see her reach out.

Altair shook her hand. "Thank you. It was my pleasure."

"What did it feel like, running around on the hull of the ship without even a space suit?" asked Faolán.

"A much more pleasant experience than I expect it would have been for anyone else aboard," said Altair in his gentle inflexion.

Ife tipped back her head and laughed, her large bosom jiggling. "Is it just me, or does this one here have a sense of humour?"

"I believe you are projecting your own sense of humour onto me," said Altair. "But I appreciate the sentiment."

Faolán laughed too and slapped Altair on the shoulder. "You're a crack-up, Big Blue."

Marcie grinned. Something had shifted in the crew, or at least amongst her friends. They were seeing Altair as a person, now that he'd done something heroic. She'd been so afraid that no one else would see him that way, but it turned out that all she'd needed to do was get herself into mortal peril!

She still didn't think they would understand if they knew she'd slept with him, though.

Marcie looked up at him sitting beside her. The lights of the mess hall caught in his long lashes and outlined his perfect cheek bones. He must have sensed her perusal, because he looked at her, his bright purple eyes flicking over her features, lingering on the yellowing bruise that was fading from her cheek, noting the bandage on her finger, looking into her eyes.

"Are you really all right?"

Beyond his shoulder, Sandeep and Ife were both noting the conversation and giving each other a laden look.

"Yes, I'm fine. Thank you."

Behind her, the door opened again. Marcie glanced, then swore under her breath and returned her attention to her meal. Simons had entered the mess hall. What was he doing there? He'd usually cleared off well before the late dinner shift.

Ife and Sandeep looked tense too, and also applied themselves to their meals as Simons got his own. There wasn't a free seat at their table, so he'd have to sit somewhere else, anyway.

But Hernandez stood. "Have a good night," he said. Marcie tried to give the midship a meaningful look, pleading in her mind, *Please stay here!* But the young man seemed unaware of the tension among the engineering crew, because he took his tray to the hatch and left without seeming aware of what he had left them to.

Simons swaggered over, tray in hand, and stared at them all. "We really sitting with that thing?" he asked, indicating Altair with his elbow.

"You could sit somewhere else," said Faolán. He didn't have to work closely with Simons, which gave him the confidence to say what the rest of them wished they could.

Simons ignored him and clanged his tray down in Hernandez's vacated space. Ife and Sandeep both started shovelling food faster into their faces. Marcie did the same. None of them would stick around for long now.

I hate this guy! thought Marcie. She'd been enjoying sitting here with her friends, having a pleasant conversation, with Altair sitting beside her, winning the crew over with his personableness. But now they were all going to cut the evening short because of Simons.

"So, what we all talkin' 'bout?" asked Simons around a mouthful of food.

"The dangerous spacewalk you sent Lieutenant Martin-Palmer on, where she had no backup," said Altair, without missing a beat.

Faolán snorted, and Marcie hid a grin behind her hand.

Simons glowered at Altair. "So that's what you're here for, huh, android? To stir up dissent among our crew?"

"No. But I find it interesting that even you find sending someone out on a dangerous spacewalk to be worthy of dissent."

"I thought Chaudhary would do the walk."

"That's no better," said Marcie. She looked at Sandeep, who had a pinched look about him, but who was otherwise staring intently at his meal. "Why would it have been any safer for Sandeep to go out alone?"

It seemed Simons wasn't willing to say the quiet part out loud. "Whatever," he shrugged. "You all think it's safe to be sitting here having a meal with an android that could go psycho and kill you all at any moment?"

As still as Altair always was, she could somehow tell he was frozen in shock at Simons' words. Marcie squared her shoulders. Simons could talk smack about her all he wanted, but not Altair, her precious, traumatised android with too gentle a nature for this sort of vitriol. "You're out of line, sir. Altair would never. He's a lovely person. He saved me today."

Simons narrowed his eyes at Marcie, then at Altair. "Don't get attached to it, lieutenant. We'll be putting it back where it came from tomorrow."

It. Marcie was livid. She didn't want to spend a single moment more with this arsehole of a man. She scooped the rest of her salad into her mouth. Ife and Sandeep also finished their meals. Faolán had been finished even before Marcie arrived. Their group rose as one and put their trays through the hatch. Altair rose with them, not at all left behind by the sudden change.

"Lieutenant Kikelomo," called out Simons as their group headed for the door. Ife stopped for a moment. "I want you at your station early tomorrow. We need to finish the hull patching ASAP."

"Aye, sir." Ife's voice whipped out.

"Oh, and android?" Altair looked back at him, as did Marcie. Simons pointed at Altair. "I can take androids like you down without breaking a sweat. I don't care how strong you are: everyone has a weakness. Keep that in mind."

Neither of them dignified that with a retort. The posturing buffoon!

Their group of five stopped in the hallway, silent for a moment.

"That mouldy old pineapple has no idea how close he came to death," said Ife. "Between me wanting to wring his neck for implying that Sandeep's disposable, and Marcie wanting to wring his neck for calling her friend an 'it'—"

"And me wanting to wring his neck for sanctioning the dangerous spacewalk in the first place," interjected Sandeep.

"He's very lucky," continued Ife. "Very lucky indeed."

"Yeah, I think Big Blue here was the only one who *wasn't* about to go terminator on his arse," said Faolán. "My condolences, friends, for having such a horrible section chief."

"Thanks," said Ife. "I'm going to bed now. I have an early start. What we doing with this one?" She pointed at Altair.

"I have it sorted," said Faolán. "We've got a place set up as a recharge station. Mayor Sirius gave the captain some guidelines."

"Have a good night, all," said Sandeep. "I still have a few diagnostics to run."

"Do you need help?" asked Marcie, concerned about leaving the last of the work to him.

"After the day you've had? Marcie, get some rest."

Ife and Sandeep both waved and headed off in different directions.

"This way, Big Blue," said Faolán. "I'll show you to your recharge station."

"Can I walk you?" asked Marcie.

"Want to know where I'm putting him?" asked Faolán.

Marcie shrugged.

The three of them walked down to deck 8. Faolán pointed along the hallway to where a security officer stood outside what Marcie knew was a cupboard. "In there?" asked Marcie.

"Mayor Sirius said they recharge standing up. And security's needed not only to protect us, but also him. What if Simons got drunk and took his aggression out on Altair while he was recharging? We have a duty of care."

It made sense. But Marcie wanted to talk to Altair, and she couldn't do so in a cupboard with a guard standing outside. "Can I have a bit of time with Altair first? I want to thank him for saving me. I've barely had a chance."

Faolán's eyebrows rose. "Uh..."

"Please. He'll be going away again soon." She was afraid Faolán would read too much into her request. But what else was she to do? She wasn't ready to end her time with Altair yet.

Faolán looked back and forth between Marcie and Altair, who stood watching the exchange.

"I shouldn't really, but..." He walked over to the security guard. "You can go take a break, Ensign Latu. We're bringing him in much later than I said I would, and I bet you've been standing here for ages. Have you had dinner?"

"No, lieutenant," she said.

"I'll ping you back in an hour. We'll do another quick walk-around, and I should have him in there recharging by the time you get back."

"Roger that." The security guard left, her back sagging with relief. She had a bit of a limp as she walked, perhaps an injury from when the ship was damaged.

Faolán led them up to the crew quarters. "Don't tell anyone I did this, though I suppose anyone who checks the security feeds would know. I'm going to let you two have a wee chat in your quarters. I'll come bang on the door when you're out of time. You'd better say whatever remains unsaid between you, 'coz we're all going to be busy tomorrow. And I *do not want to know*, got it?"

Marcie's cheeks burned. He knew. Or he suspected. He was looking the other way, though, and that would have to do. This was it for her and Altair. She'd be too busy doing her job from tomorrow, and the *Sunda Tiger* probably wouldn't linger long now since there were no human colonists to reconnect with. They'd be reporting back, and then a delegation of android specialists would come to replace them. So Marcie just nodded and led Altair into her cabin.

The door whooshed shut behind them. The soundproofing was good in these cabins, so they would be in full privacy now. Marcie tagged the lock and took one step into the middle of her minuscule standing area. Altair stood with his back to the door, looking around. Marcie turned and waved her hands around. "Well, this is where I live."

"It is compact."

"Not much bigger than the cupboard they're putting you in, eh?" Marcie sat on her bunk, and Altair leaned past her to look out her tiny porthole, the perfect curve of his arse right in front of her face. The view from Marcie's cabin was of the space side, just an endless expanse of stars.

"The cabin is small, but the view is infinite," he said.

"Yeah." Marcie was pleased he saw the appeal. She patted the bunk beside her, and he sat down.

"You said you wanted to thank me. You do not have to. It was no bother at all to come out and aid you today."

Marcie smiled. There were still things that slid past him, the more subtle threads of conversation. She knew she had to be more literal with him; she just hadn't wanted to be in public.

"'Thanking' is sometimes used as a euphemism. I want to thank you by doing something with you, not just with my words."

Altair's violet eyes shone brighter in the dim night light of her cabin. "What do you want to do with me?"

"I want to see if we can uncover another one of those memories for you. It may be our last opportunity." She motioned to the narrow bunk. "Think you'd fit on here with me?"

"Only if we lay one on top of the other."

"That's what I was hoping."

CHAPTER 22

Marcie reached for him. There was something vulnerable about her. As she stroked a warm hand over his shirt-clad chest, up his shoulder, his neck, he thought about how pale and scared her face had been inside that space helmet. How the vacuum that had not bothered him much had been such a danger to her. She was so fragile. So precious. She had nearly been lost that day. Every moment in her continued presence was a gift.

"Your skin feels different," she said, a crease marring her brow.

"The vacuum made it age. I will requisition a new epidermis when I return to the surface. Do you like this colour? Should I choose a new one?" Altair had never thought to ask for anyone else's opinion of his appearance.

She knelt on the bunk and pulled the hem of his black t-shirt up, exposing his midsection. "I love this colour." She leaned down and licked his stomach.

Altair wanted to take his time with Marcie, but Lieutenant O'Donoghue would not wait forever. He pulled the shirt off and placed it on Marcie's table, so close to the bunk it was in easy reach. She moved her mouth up his body and licked his nipple. His extra programming must include secondary erogenous zones, because his lower spine tingled and his penis grew hard without him giving it a specific command to do so. He simply responded to her ministrations like a real human would.

Marcie ran a hand over the bulge he was causing in the trousers. He did not like the fabric separating them. He lifted his hips and pulled the trousers off, his growing hardness springing free.

"That's it," said Marcie. She stood and unzipped her suit, flinging it off. Now wearing just a tank top and underwear, she crawled onto the bunk and pushed Altair towards the angled wall that was a part of the hull. "Scoot over there."

Altair put his back to the wall. A strange floating sensation overtook his torso. "There is no gravity at this end. My upper body feels no gravity, while my lower body does."

"Your head and shoulders are off the edge of the gravity plating. It's an interesting sensation. Best way to have a mind-blowing orgasm on a ship. Mind you, I'm usually doing it by myself."

"You sit here and..."

"Touch myself, yes. That's right where I do it. And now I'm going to touch you." She knelt between his thighs and took him in hand, starting with a leisurely stroke. "How's this?"

At her touch, the electrical signals in his body went haywire. "Yes. Perfect."

She grinned up at him, the corners of her eyes crinkling. Then she cupped his simulated testicles with her other hand, keeping her bandaged, sore finger held away. "And this?"

The sensation up his spine changed in pitch. "Yes."

"And this?" She leaned forward and took him into her mouth.

Altair could only gasp. She'd done this to him before in the shower, and it was just as pleasurable this time as then. She looked up at him as she bobbed her head up and down on him, and he clenched the sheet in his fist. The tiny room filled with sounds that Altair could hardly believe he was involved in: the wet sound of her mouth on him, and his own gasps that sounded far more human than he usually did. How was it like this? Who had programmed him this way? Did it matter? Should he just enjoy the benefit of his unusual, unknown past?

Did anything matter as much as the fact that he was here now with Marcie, being pleasured by her?

His body tightened, and Marcie must have been able to read the change in him, because she moved faster, sucked harder. He groaned, actually groaned, as his synapses fired in a conflagration of lust. He bucked, stilled, and that strange sound emanated from deep within him...

...a town meeting of humans...

...a biologist holding up fish caught from the lake, demonstrating the biodiversity gain and how well the terraformation had taken...

...holding two human children, one on each shoulder, as he walked through rain and floodwater that ran between the temporary houses of the first, abandoned 227C camp...

He loosened and gasped, his hair floating about his forehead in the zero-g pocket.

Marcie sat back on her heels before him, wiping the smeared saliva from around her mouth, her eyes twinkling in the low light. "Did you see anything?"

"I did. Just fragments, but... we used to have a settlement at another beach on the lake. We moved after floods damaged the settlement in the second summer. I do not believe we had records of such a move. It would be news to the colony."

Marcie's face lit up. "That's something you could verify if you could find the right location."

"Indeed. Thank you."

Marcie blushed. "Well, I wanted to do that before you left. To show my appreciation. Just in case, well." It seemed Marcie was thinking of how their time together was ending. "Do you want to get back to the recharge station now?"

"No."

"No?" She sounded breathless. Hopeful.

"Lieutenant O'Donoghue mentioned an hour. We've used less than ten minutes." Altair sat up and looked Marcie in the eye. "I want to show my appreciation too. You have no idea of the value of what you have given me over these last few days."

Marcie flushed a deeper red and gasped as he held her by the hips, swivelled, and put her down where he had been reclining. Her knees fell apart, the damp patch in the gusset of her underwear visible. Altair hooked his fingers into the sides of her panties and dragged them down over her legs. Her breath hitched. She wedged her upper body into the zero-g part of her room and looked down her body at him, her eyelids half lowered and her breathing deep and rapid.

Again, Altair wished he could take time with her pleasure, but they had to hurry. He parted the folds beneath her wet curls, leaned down, and kissed her there. She moaned and her thighs clenched around his ears. She had a thick musk, as she had not yet washed the fear-sweat from her body, but he did not mind because it was all her: her emotions, her flesh, her passion. He looked up past the gentle mounds of her chest to her open, gasping mouth, her hair waving around in the zero-g like it was underwater. With so much of her body weightless, one hand on her hip was all he needed to nudge her up into the air so he could move his face closer in. He kissed her deep and felt her moan all around him. His excited body responded again, standing to attention.

He lost himself in the rhythm he had discovered in her their first time, delving into the places she liked to be touched the best, at the pace that drove her closer, then eased back, and closer, then back again. She gripped his hair and pulled him closer still, demanding that he not back off this time. As much as it must have frustrated her, it worked: when she orgasmed, she orgasmed hard, gasping his name and riding his face for many long moments. Her body fluids dripped down his chin onto the bunk.

Still gasping from her release, Marcie whipped off the tank top she wore, the last piece of clothing between them, and encircled him with her legs. He let his penis vibrate and rubbed the tip against her, and brushed one nipple with a finger, thinking to revive her arousal that way, but her body's demands had returned faster than he expected. She grabbed two handfuls of his buttocks and pulled him towards her. "Altair, I need you inside me. Now." She was already tilting her hips, positioning herself for him.

He slipped forward with no resistance into her wet warmth. The tingles started again straight away. He knew he would be orgasming again within her.

They slapped together, their sounds more obscene than ever before. They half floated together, her moans and her breath a cloud from which he never wanted to escape. Her fingers dug into him in such a way that he was sure their lovemaking would be visible as rents in his silicone skin. Thankfully, he was already going to replace it, or he'd be flaunting her passion for a long time to come.

She grabbed his hand and put it to one breast. He massaged the nipple. "Harder," she demanded. "More." He applied more pressure. "More, please." Her passion made him feel mighty, made him feel real. He leaned down as his hips continued to move, taking her nipple in his teeth. He bit down, hard enough to hurt but not injure. "Ngh!" It was enough to tip her over the edge, and she came again.

Then Altair's body began to tighten and buck, an instinct he could barely believe he had within him taking over. That telltale feeling rose in his lower spine, in his abdomen. And then he was gasping her name into her neck, as he pounded into her and stilled, and she held him through it.

...a human woman with dark, curly hair ticking a sheet on a clipboard...

...his red penis, erect and lubricated, slipping against a brown-pink human one, red and tanned hands tangled together around the two erections...

...screams and smoke...

He came to, lying on his back on Marcie's bunk. She was propped up on her elbow, running a hand through his hair. "More memories?"

Her tender ministrations almost made him forget she was aware he was not a human. It did not seem to matter to her what he was, and he felt exceedingly grateful for that fact. "Yes. So many memories. I lived a whole life before I became myself. I thought all those memory records were gone, but they are all there."

"But you still can't access them by choice?"

He looked up at her, silhouetted against the light above her desk. She was not asking idly; there was professional curiosity in her voice. "That is correct. I do not know how to access these memories at will."

"Hmm, something about one system overriding another, I suppose..." She patted him on the chest. "We'd better get dressed again, in case Faolán returns."

They were mostly dressed when Marcie received a comms. She answered. "Sandeep? What's up?"

"Marcie, you need to get to the mess hall right now. Something's happening."

Marcie frowned. "What's going on?"

"It's not good, Marcie. Bring your friend. And prepare yourself. This is going to be hard. On both of you."

CHAPTER 23

When they emerged from Marcie's cabin, Faolán was already heading their way. He skidded to a stop and then joined them as they went to the mess hall.

"Do you know what's going on?" asked Marcie. Her belly was roiling. Sandeep had sounded so worried.

"No. Lieutenant Chaudhary didn't have time to brief me. Just said to hurry."

As they strode along the hallway, more people emerged from their cabins.

"What's going on?" asked Ensign Fisher as he exited his cabin in front of them.

"Dunno," said Faolán. "What do you know?"

"There's a message on the message board from LC Simons. Says to come to the mess hall for evidence the androids are up to no good." His eyes flicked beyond Marcie's shoulder. When he noted Altair's presence, his eyes widened, and he turned and hurried away from them towards the mess hall.

Simons. Marcie felt sick. What had he done?

They followed, joining the straggle of crew members who had responded to Simons' summons. Marcie looked over her shoulder and gave Altair a reassuring smile as they went. Whatever information Simons was claiming to have must be fake. How could he have any sort of proof of anything nefarious?

When they entered the mess hall, there were already about twenty people there, including Sandeep, Fisher, Gagnon, and, of course, Simons. Faolán went straight to Sandeep and whispered in his ear, but Marcie stood frozen just inside the door with Altair at her back, her mouth gaping.

Simons stood at the head of the room, in the place where people stood when leading social events. "...This cannot be tolerated," he was saying in an impassioned voice. "How can we believe this is anything other than seduction for the purposes of industrial espionage?" On the projector behind him was a still image taken inside her own cabin, just a short while ago, in what they had thought was a private moment. There, for everyone to see, was Marcie in a side-on view, wearing nothing but her tank top, Altair's blue hand covering her hip, and his face buried between her legs. His naked form was fully visible.

Marcie gasped, and her knees buckled. Altair grabbed her elbow and held her upright until she could take her own weight again.

"Speak of the devil: here it is now!" said Simons.

Everyone in the mess hall turned to look at them. Marcie looked at the expressions turned her way. Sandeep looked worried, Faolán faintly guilty. There was one thoughtful face in the back. But everyone else looked some variation of shocked or disgusted. Gagnon, who had made her opinions abundantly clear before, even spat.

Marcie turned her eyes back to Simons. She wanted to smash the smug grin off his face. "What the actual fuck?" She jabbed a finger at the display. "Why is that up there? What do you think you're doing?"

"That's what we should say to you, don't you think? What were *you* doing?"

"Nothing I do in the privacy of my cabin is anyone else's business. Get that down, now!" She glowered at the crowd. "And the rest of you: have you no shame?" Behind her, Marcie could hear more people entering the mess hall.

"Come on, now, Martin-Palmer!" said Simons. "I chose a tasteful angle so we can't see any of your bits."

"What about him?" said Marcie, waving a hand at Altair. "You didn't choose a 'tasteful' angle for Altair!"

Simons scoffed. "That's not a person. And anyway, we've all heard how the androids don't wear clothes down there. What does it matter?"

Marcie gritted her teeth. "What he does at home has no bearing on this. You've violated our privacy, Simons!"

"Is this the fabled human kindness?" asked Altair. "If so, it leaves much to be desired." There was a nervous shuffling of feet around the room at his words.

Then Ife stepped up from behind and stood beside Marcie. "Turn it off, Simons."

Sandeep also stepped up and stood on Marcie's other side. Faolán walked towards Simons, his hand out. "Hand over the remote," he said, but Simons held his hand behind his back.

"What's going on in here?" cracked out an authoritative voice. They all turned to see Captain Rodriguez and Commander Mori standing in the doorway, surveying events. The captain's eyes narrowed when she saw the image Simons was displaying.

"Lieutenant Commander Simons, explain," said the captain as she walked into the middle of the room.

"The android is a security concern, and here is the evidence. It's seduced one of our engineers, probably to get vital information."

Captain Rodriguez pursed her lips. She glanced only briefly at the image. "Lieutenant Martin-Palmer, did you consent to this image being shown to the crew?"

"No, captain."

"Altair? How about you?"

"I did not."

Captain Rodriguez looked at Commander Mori, then nodded at the screen. The commander strode over to Simons and grabbed the controller out of his hand, then turned the screen off.

"How did he even get the image?" asked Sandeep in a quiet voice that nonetheless carried throughout the room. "Does he have spy gear in her cabin?"

All the blood drained from Marcie's face and she felt like she was going to be sick. "How long has he been spying on me?" she whispered. She'd thought to check for spy gear when she first went down to 227C. She'd never even considered that she'd need to do so in her own cabin.

Captain Rodriguez glared at Simons. "That's a good question. Lieutenants Yu and Darzi, escort Simons to the brig."

"But, captain! What about the android? I was just—"

"Whatever you thought you were doing," said the captain, her dark eyes as hard as stone, "doesn't make up for how you recorded a female crew member in her private cabin and then distributed voyeuristic pornographic content to the crew without her consent or anyone else's. At the very least, you'll face a Court Martial when we return to Sol."

"Don't you know who my father is?" yelled Simons, his face contorted. Marcie looked around the room. There were some scowls directed at Simons now. Maybe some of them had forgotten until that moment how he got his position.

"I don't care," said the captain. "Take him away."

The captain then turned to Marcie. "Is there anyone you would trust to go into your cabin and look for whatever he recorded this with?"

"Lieutenant Kikelomo," she said.

"Kikelomo? Could you search Martin-Palmer's quarters please? Remove any illicit tech you find, and bag it to preserve fingerprints. Is it OK, Lieutenant Martin-Palmer, if Commander Mori goes too?"

Marcie nodded.

After the security lieutenants had taken Simons away and Ife and Commander Mori had left for their task, the captain eyed the rest of the crew in the mess hall. "As for the rest of you, you're dismissed. I encourage you to do some soul-searching in your private time. Only one crew member contacted me about what was going on. What were the rest of you thinking? Off you go. Martin-Palmer and O'Donoghue, please stay. You too, Altair."

When just the four of them stood in the room, Marcie shuffled awkwardly, and looked up at Altair. He looked as placid as ever, but the way he was looking at her, she was sure he was concerned about her.

She looked at the captain's inscrutable face. "Captain, I—"

The captain held up her hand. "I'm not waiting for an explanation," she said. "O'Donoghue, take Altair to his recharge alcove and make sure he's safely guarded."

"Captain—" said Marcie.

"This is for Altair's safety as well as our own. What if Simons has incited some of the crew to violence? Altair will be safer under guard." The captain turned to Altair. "Will you go willingly?"

"Yes, captain, I will," he said. "So long as Marcie is not left alone, either."

Marcie's lip wobbled at his concern.

"I will take charge of Lieutenant Martin-Palmer myself," said the captain.

Faolán, looking relieved, and far quieter than Marcie had ever seen him, led Altair away. Altair looked back at Marcie as he left the mess hall, and Marcie gave him an encouraging smile. She would explain everything she had to so that Altair would not get in trouble.

"Please, come with me to my office," said the captain.

Marcie followed her captain through the halls of the ship. Even though it was late, there were people about, and everyone seemed to know. The captain gave anyone who stared at Marcie a hard look, and they moved along.

When they entered the office, Marcie stood to attention, but the captain waved her to a seat. "Tea? Coffee?" she asked. "Something stronger?"

"Oh, um, a tea would be lovely." Marcie's knee began jiggling as soon as she sat, and she chewed on a thumbnail. Her stomach still roiled, threatening to spill her dinner.

Captain Rodriguez spent a few minutes at her personal kitchen nook and then brought two steaming mugs to the large glass desk. She took a seat across from Marcie, and a sip of her drink. Marcie took a sip of her own, even though it was too hot, to cover her nervousness and to settle her stomach.

"You know, as a captain, I have not only a duty of care to the mission, but also to my crew. As such, you and I need to have a very uncomfortable conversation. I want to apologise in advance if I touch on any upsetting topics. I also want to assure you that anything you say in here, I will keep in strictest confidence. OK?"

"Yes, captain. Understood."

"May I call you Marcie for this conversation? You can call me Robin, or captain, if that feels uncomfortable for you. Whatever you like."

"You can call me Marcie. I'm not sure I can bring myself to be that informal, though."

The captain smiled. "That's fine. Right then, Marcie. I want to get the most uncomfortable bit out of the way first. There's no debating that Simons has violated your privacy most egregiously. But there remains the question of Altair. Was the, ah, activity in your cabin consensual? Were you pressured at all?"

Marcie was caught between wanting to defend Altair from the accusation, and wanting to cry in relief about the captain being so concerned for her welfare. She wiped a tear away and sniffed. "It was consensual, captain. Altair did nothing wrong."

The captain breathed in a sigh of relief. "Good; that's good. That was my main lingering concern. How we deal with this situation going forward would be different, depending on whether it was consensual or non-consensual." She took a long gulp of her drink. "I'm not going to ask why or how it started, because that's none of my business. And goodness knows, there's no Orion Navy rule against relations with colonists on missions. I guess this might explain why you were finding your assigned android to be 'amiable,' though, huh?"

Marcie blushed.

"I'll have to ask Altair if he too considers the activity to be consensual. What do you think he'd say?"

Marcie took a sip of her tea while gathering her thoughts. "We had a conversation about that. Um, before. Because I had some concerns about the ability of an android to consent when programming may interfere. He was adamant that he can consent. And he did."

The captain nodded. "OK. Let's leave the issue of consent for now. I'm not going to ask why you risked being intimate with him here on the ship, either. You must have thought it might be the last chance you had to spend private time together. I can understand that. And I'm not going to ask why you considered an android to be a potential partner, coz', hey, I got eyes in my head. I just want to ask: what do you want to do now? How would you like to proceed?"

Marcie ran a hand through her hair, probably messing it up even more than it already was. "I want to know what Simons did, how long he was spying on me. The thought that he might've been watching me get dressed, sleeping, and whatnot all along makes me feel like I'm going to hurl. I want to know how bad it is. I won't know what to do until I know that."

"The commander will be looking into that right now. She'll come here to report to me."

Marcie nodded and smiled. It was inspiring how the captain knew that without checking in with the commander first. The two women had been working together for years and were perfectly in synch.

"While we wait for their report, why don't you tell me more about your thoughts on 227C and what you observed there?"

Marcie spent a while telling the captain about the things she had seen on the surface: what the Welcome Centre was like, the Quartermaster, the familiars and Delichon, which she knew she was going to miss. And things about Altair, too. It was cathartic to speak about him without having to hold back, hiding the true nature of her feelings, to speak about how considerate he'd been, how impressive the gardens he had curated were, how he had walked along the beach with her and talked about his fears. She probably sounded like a love-sick youth, and that was OK. It was all out in the open now. And the captain didn't judge. She just smiled and nodded along.

A chime sounded, and the captain tapped her sleek glass desk. "Yes?"

"Commander Mori and Lieutenant Kikelomo, here to report, captain."

"Come in."

The two women entered. Commander Mori was carrying a small magnetic bottle with a tiny device in it.

"What did you find?" asked the captain.

"We removed a device from the underside of Martin-Palmer's desk. It's a recording device."

It was exactly what Marcie was expecting they would find, and yet seeing it in the commander's hand made her feel woozy. Ife stepped closer and squeezed Marcie's shoulder before stepping back into place. Marcie gave her a weak smile.

"Anything else? Did you find how long it was there?" asked the captain.

"We looked into the security feeds, and we have some good news on that front," said the commander. "Simons broke into Martin-Palmer's cabin and placed the device while we were on the planet's surface, taking the opportunity while she was away. It seems that, while he intended to record her over time, he hadn't had a chance to yet. That one recording will be the only one he took."

Marcie sighed. It was obviously not great that he'd seen anything at all, but Marcie's fears of Simons having dozens of recordings of Marcie undressed in her cabin had thankfully not eventuated.

"Well, that's something, at least," said the captain.

"It means that Simons' original aim had nothing to do with the androids, though, captain," said Ife.

"I concur. No matter what, he will not be having a continued career with the Orion Navy, I assure you. He thinks he's immune because of his connections, as if other people don't have shoulders they can tap." The captain drained the last of her beverage. "Good work, team. Let's keep the evidence safe and sort it all out when we're back at Sol."

"Roger that, captain," said the commander. "I'll—"

A sudden jolt cut her off, followed by a loud bang. Marcie clung to her bolted-down chair to keep from being thrown to the floor. Her mug went flying, smashing in a puddle of tea on the wall. The tea didn't fall. Drops spun across the room as globules, as Marcie drifted out of her chair. Ife caught the back of it as she, too, drifted.

Captain Rodriguez hooked her heels under her own chair and dragged herself back to her desk. She slapped a palm down. "Status report!" she barked.

"Explosion in the hangar bay, captain. The engines are also non-responsive."

She looked up at where Marcie and Ife clung to the chair. "Get to engineering, stat. Get me that engine back online. Martin-Palmer, you have Simons' place."

"Roger that, captain," said Marcie. She and Ife both pushed off as one, heading out the door.

What had happened in the mess hall would have to wait.

"I'm so sorry, Big Blue. I don't want to lock you in, but..."

"It is no bother, Lieutenant O'Donoghue. Your captain is right: this is a precaution against harm to me as well as harm by me."

Also, Altair did not know what would happen if a human attacked him. He did not want to hurt anyone. But he had already discovered two surprising pieces of specialist coding within him he had not been aware of. He could not be sure that he did not possess some unknown self-defence coding. Altair could very well be the exact danger that Simons had implied he was.

"Please lock me in as your captain ordered."

The lieutenant took a breath. "OK. I'll be here until I'm relieved of duty, but I have two officers I trust scheduled to relieve me in a while. I'll see you in the morning, no matter what."

"Understood. Please get some rest."

The door swooshed shut. Altair was alone in the small cubicle, lit only by a dim light overhead. He found the charging pad, repurposed from an equipment charging point. He ought to charge, but he was not ready to sleep yet. So much had happened...

Was Marcie all right? What happened was awful. He never again wanted to see a mix of such emotions on her face. Simons was everything the androids of 227C feared about humans. If someone like that had been their first contact, Vega would have felt vindicated in his distrust.

Altair turned the events of the evening over and over in his memory banks for a long minute, trying to make sense of it all. Wondering how he would need to report it to Sirius. But he had to stop for now, and leave the processing for later. What if someone came for him? He needed power. He attached the charging pad and slid towards oblivion...

...

He jolted awake. The ship shook around him and the gravity failed. He checked his internal clock and found he had been charging for less than an hour. Sirens blared beyond the door.

Marcie. Was she well? What happened? Had she run to fix whatever disaster had occurred? Experience indicated the probability was high.

Altair disengaged the charging pad. Whatever power he had gained so far would have to do. He banged on the door. "Hello? What is happening? Lieutenant O'Donoghue?"

For a long minute, there was no answer. He banged and called again, but there was no response. Had O'Donoghue left him behind? Or was he hurt?

Finally, the door swooshed open. Lieutenant O'Donoghue clung to the doorway, blood beading from a gash on his forehead and encroaching on his eye. The lieutenant brushed the blood away, and it floated as globules in zero gravity. "Wha' happened?" he asked.

"I was going to ask you the same thing."

"There was a bang. I think I was knocked out. How long was I out?"

"By my calculation, 1.31 minutes."

"What happened to the gravity?"

"I am unaware."

"Yeah, I know. Rhetorical question."

They were startled by a loud voice over the communications system. "All personnel on decks 7 and 8, relocate to deck 6 or get into a space suit and a closed room. Hull structural integrity is failing in your zone."

"That's just great," said O'Donoghue.

They were on deck 8.

Altair took a quick look at the lieutenant. The man's eyes were crossed, and he had not attempted to relocate yet. Altair considered the possibility that O'Donoghue had received a debilitating concussion to be high. Altair took a deep breath in case the air would be needed for other lungs, magnetised his feet, and slung the man onto his back. Then he ran.

He ran along the corridor and to a turn that led towards a staircase up to the next deck. In that shorter corridor, he came across the limping security officer, Ensign Latu. She was clipped to a rail on the wall and pulling herself along hand over hand. She heard his approach and looked behind. Her eyes widened at his appearance, and she pointed a handheld weapon at him. "Freeze!"

Altair slowed and held up a hand. "The lieutenant has a concussion. I have magnetised feet. Let me help you."

The ensign warred with herself for a moment. Then she unclipped. Altair slung his free arm around her waist and continued running, taking the stairs ahead three at a time. As they approached a bulkhead door, a whooshing sensation tried to pull him back. Depressurisation.

"It's gonna close!" yelled the ensign.

Altair sped up. He ran faster than he had known was possible. He whipped past the bulkhead, only for the door to slam closed behind him.

One more floor to go.

He didn't pause to think. He started running up the next flight.

Whoosh. Slide. Depressurisation.

But this time, they were further from the bulkhead at the top.

Altair leapt. He saw the bulkhead approach as if in slow motion. The doors began to slide. Digging in with one foot, he threw the two humans he carried, hoping they would not hit the far wall too hard. They cleared the bulkhead—

—slam—

WHOOSH.

He tumbled end-over-end down the stairs and along the corridor. A hole gaped at the far end of the corridor, the stars solid pinpricks of light beyond.

He would fall for hours until he burned up on reentry, just like his trousers.

He stretched his arm out and caught a railing.

The metal shivered, but held.

The air rushing past him lessened and then was gone. Altair remagnetised to the deck and walked over to the hole. He even retained his clothing this time (he had learned the importance of tying the drawstring waist tightly). Now the deck was depressurised, the ship felt still to him, but the view outside showed otherwise. The stars slid by, then the planet, then stars again. The ship was in a spin. Not enough to make the centripetal force obvious, but enough that the ship must be adrift. Finally, he noticed that the vibration of the engine that had been present throughout the ship the whole time he was aboard was absent.

The *Sunda Tiger* was not only in a spin. It was in a spin with no engine to correct.

Marcie. She would go down with the ship if he did nothing. But Marcie would not be in the depressurised part of the ship.

What if she was lost at depressurisation? What if she is freezing in space?

No.

No, that will not be.

But the problem remained: how could Altair get back into the parts of the ship where the humans were? He could not force a door without risking people on the other side.

Altair hung outside the hole and looked along the hull of the ship for an idea. Further aft, a bulge was forming on another portion of deck seven. Another section was about to depressurise.

How much power could Altair put into his legs if he had time to prepare for it? Could he run against the drag of depressurising air and get to the next door before it slammed shut?

If he kept his feet magnetised and avoided being blown out into space, he would at the very least be no worse off than he already was.

Altair climbed out and ran along the hull to stand beside the bulging plating. He braced and sent as much power to his legs as he could.

The hull popped. As soon as the debris cleared, Altair ran. He got his hand around a rail just in case and pumped his legs with all his power. His feet slipped. He gained again.

He was lucky in that a bulkhead was just ahead of him. But the door flashed and began to close. Altair dug deep into all of his reserves. He was head through, hips through...

The sensors in his left leg went wild. Air screamed through a narrow gap. A gap the width of his calf. Altair looked at his leg caught in the door. He hoped no humans had got caught like this, because it was hard even on his body. Altair put his free leg against the door for leverage and yanked. His leg came free, and the bulkhead slammed properly closed. Unfortunately, much of the silicone skin of his lower leg remained on the other side. His metal workings glinted in the light, some of them looking buckled. He had no time to inspect the damage.

Now he was back in the pressurised portion of the ship, he could hear the alarms as they continued to blare. He started running again, now with a limp. He had to get up to deck six or higher and find his way back to engineering, the most likely place to find Marcie.

He made it to deck six, but his journey aft to engineering was hard to navigate. Portions of deck six had also depressurised, and he had to double back to find a clear route twice. On his third attempt, he saw two humans ahead of him in the hallway, making their way through zero gravity in panicked movements.

"Do you need help?" he called. They looked back. It was a security guard and Simons.

The security guard reacted as Ensign Latu had. "Freeze!"

He had picked the wrong person as the bigger threat.

As soon as the security guard turned his back on Simons, the larger blond man grabbed a truncheon from the guard's belt and hit him over the head.

Altair startled at the display of cruelty. Was the human all right? The blow looked dangerous. He sped forward to check on the attacked human. "What are you doing?" he said to Simons. "The ship is in freefall. Where would you escape to?"

"Oh, we've still got a good hour," said Simons. He grabbed the laser weapon from the guard's belt and waved it wildly, shooting laser bolts in random directions.

Altair was ready to grab Simons' hand if he looked like he would shoot him. But the man was shooting wide, and Altair was in no danger.

Or so he thought.

When a bolt ricocheted off a panel behind him and hit him on the back of the neck, he realised he too had underestimated Simons.

Altair could not move. His body simply did not respond.

Simons grinned at him. "I told you I could take you out, didn't I? Fun fact: all you androids have a spot right here where you're vulnerable." He pointed to his own neck. "It's a weakness borne of trying too much to look like humans, and having a narrow neck carrying a lot of information."

Altair tried to respond, but even his mouth was unresponsive. Was this permanent, or would his ability to move return in a moment?

"I knew you were here for sabotage," said Simons. "You wouldn't have done this to the ship without a way of getting tech off, so there must be a way to get the engine going again. You're going to tell me."

Altair wanted to tell the man that he was not responsible for the damage to the ship, but he could not.

Simons grabbed Altair by his hair and began dragging him down the hallway, one hand on the railing. Altair could do nothing but watch the ceiling drift by overhead. Simons took him down a corridor, around a corner, up a flight of stairs, and to a door. He tagged the door open and drifted Altair into a dim room, locking the door behind them. When Simons threw a tie around him and lashed him to a surface, he tilted enough that he could see they were in some kind of engineering lab.

Simons moved about the room, causing clinks and clangs. Then he drifted over, tools on his belt and in his hands. "Now, let's get you talking."

CHAPTER 25

The scream of sirens cut through Marcie's skull as she dug around in the bowels of the engine. She wiped sweat off her brow. She kept drifting to the base of the tube she was inspecting and then hoisting herself up again. The ship was in a slow spin, enough to create a very slight pseudo-gravity.

Diagnostic complete, she shut the hatch and pushed off to rejoin the others. "Status report," she said to the room at large.

"We've got one crazy virus here in the computers," said Sandeep. "I've never seen anything like it. It'll take hours to pick out all the functions it's affecting."

"We don't have hours, Sandeep."

He looked up at Marcie. Fear shone in his dark eyes. "I know."

Marcie took a deep breath. "Ife? Thoughts?"

Ife shrugged her shoulders. "I can't find a single thing that will override this virus and get us going. The worst part is the magnetic bottle. The virus is changing the parameters on an unpredictable schedule. If I had some time to run the calculations, I could pick a window where we could safely turn it on, but..."

"But we don't have that kind of time."

"Correct." Ife closed her eyes. "All I'd do if I pushed it would be blow us up. Anything down in the antimatter insertion point look promising, sir?"

Marcie felt a jolt at being referred to as 'sir' by her friend. "The opposite."

"What now?" asked Sandeep.

Marcie gulped. "The machinery down there is starting to run hot."

"Fuck," said Ife. The three other engineers in the room whispered among themselves: more swear words, more fear.

Marcie racked her brains. There must be something they could do. Some clever solution she could pull out of her arse. Her mother would have been able to. Her mother had saved her own Sol Corp ship multiple times in circumstances as difficult as these. She was a legend. But Marcie couldn't think of anything that could save the *Sunda Tiger*.

"Right now," she said aloud, a deep weariness settling upon her, "the only question is which will take us out first: 227C's atmosphere, or our own failing engine exploding." She looked at her two friends in turn. "There's only one thing I can do, and it's going to be a major life-changing event for everyone on board. Are you with me?"

"It's all we can do," agreed Ife. She reached out and grabbed Marcie's hand, and Sandeep took her other. "Make the call, Marcie."

They went with her to the head engineer panel and braced her against the gradual drift of centripetal force while she tapped the console. "Captain, engineering."

"Martin-Palmer, I hope you have good news for me," sounded Captain Rodriguez's voice. "We need some luck."

Marcie took a deep breath. "I'm sorry, captain, but there's nothing we can do here. We've been fully sabotaged by both mechanical and viral means. It'll take much more time than we have left to fix this. The chance we'd lose the entire crew in trying is high. I recommend you send a distress call to the Orion Navy and then give the order to abandon ship."

There was a heavy pause on the line. "Understood. Thank you for your efforts, team. I know you've done all you can. Not your fault we rolled a one today." The call cut, and then half a minute later, the captain's voice sounded over the loudspeakers. "This is the captain speaking. All hands, abandon ship. I repeat: All hands, abandon ship. Escape pods are being programmed to convene on the 227C Research Centre. May whatever you pray to shine upon you, crew of the *Sunda Tiger*."

Marcie and her friends looked at one another. "Let's go."

They abandoned engineering, closing the airlock behind them. Marcie paused outside at a panel that she never thought she would need to open. She put in her code, gave the command. In ten minutes, certain structural supports would disengage. It wouldn't be a clean break, but with any luck the dangerous engine would break away on atmospheric insertion. If the rest of the ship crashed without the engine, materials may be salvageable. If the whole ship crashed and went up in a matter/antimatter explosion, they would have nothing.

Ife squeezed her shoulder when she closed the hatch. "Let's get to an escape pod."

Marcie's stomach flipped. "You go on ahead."

"What? Marcie—" said Sandeep.

Crew members streamed past them, heading from the stairwell to the escape pods further along their corridor. Marcie looked both of her friends in the eye, let them see how determined she was. "I have to go make sure he's OK. He might be locked in his charging cubby for all I know."

"Marcie," said Ife in a gentle voice. "The charging port they made for him was down on eight. Seven and eight lost atmosphere."

Marcie's stomach flipped. "He doesn't need air."

"Maybe so, but you do. Besides, the bulkhead doors are closed. You can't help him."

"What if he wasn't there?" Tears were collecting in the corners of her eyes.

"He's not a crew member," said Sandeep. "How would you find him if he's not in the directory?"

One of the crew members streaming past them skidded to a halt, his hand squeaking on the railing. He was a security officer, and blood was budding off from a blow to his head. He looked pale and sweaty, and he struggled to focus his eyes on Marcie.

"Your android," he said.

"What? Do you know where Altair is?"

"I think Simons has him. He hit me and took my weapon."

Ife's eyebrows lowered. "Altair did?"

"No, Simons. Simons hit me. I was trying to evacuate him, the fucker."

"Up here?" asked Marcie. "Not down on the lower decks?"

"On sixth, but I think they went to fifth."

Hope flared in Marcie's chest. "Go with this guy to an escape pod, please," she said to her friends. "He looks like he needs the help. I'll see you on the surface."

"We can't persuade you otherwise, can we?" said Ife.

"Nope."

"That android must fuck like a champ."

Marcie grinned at her. "Two words for you: Vibrating. Penis."

"Ugh, TMI," said Sandeep.

Marcie waved and then pulled herself down the stairs to deck five. She belatedly realised that if something were to go wrong, the last words her friends would have ever heard her say were 'vibrating penis.' Oh, well. At least she'd make a funny anecdote for them to tell.

She stopped at a panel on fifth and pulled up the directory. With the emergency protocols in place, she could see where Simons was: right where she suspected he would be, in one of the engineering labs.

There were weapons lockers around, but she didn't have clearance to open them. Instead, Marcie ducked into the lab next to the one Simons was in and grabbed a few sharp tools to add to the ones already on her belt. The lab shared a rear fume cubby with Simons' lab. With any luck, he would look at the main door for people arriving.

Marcie pulled herself hand-over-hand into the cubby and peered through the door's glass panel into the lab next door.

The lights were dim, shining in low glints off metal racks and benches. Equipment and heavy, clunky military-grade computers designed to be static units had shifted about the room in the explosion. The debris of hasty zero-g engineering spun lazily in the air.

Altair was strapped to a table, cables snaking away from him to several computer units. For a heart-rending moment, Marcie thought Simons had pulled the cables out of Altair. If he was already gone... But they seemed to be cables he'd attached to Altair. Marcie felt faint with relief. But Altair was not safe yet, not by a long shot.

Simons himself was changing settings on a display and talking to Altair. His back was to Marcie. While she watched, he floated over to another piece of machinery that was magnetised to the floor, dug his heels in, and started dragging it closer. Though she couldn't hear it yet, she felt sure that Simons must be causing a racket. It was her chance to enter the room.

Marcie pushed the door release button, slipped through, and shut it again. She dived behind a storage unit and grabbed a hold of its lower edge to hold her head down. She held her breath and listened, trying to hear if Simons had heard her. But he was still struggling with the unit, trying to get the right leverage off a nearby railing and grunting with effort.

Marcie peered round the corner. Altair didn't seem to be conscious. His body was immobile and his face slack, eyes closed. His left lower leg had also received some awful trauma, with part of his trouser leg torn away to show the extent of the damage. It looked like something had ripped the silicone skin off, exposing the workings within. If a human's leg had been degloved like that, it would be a life-altering injury.

Marcie ducked behind the unit as Simons turned, another cable in his hand. "All right, fucker. You won't lock me out this time," he muttered. "See if you can avoid showing me your transcript." There was a scraping noise, some taps on a terminal.

Marcie risked looking again. Simons had attached another cable and was scrolling through a screen that displayed lines of code. "Good encoding, but not good enough. This is a fucking hyper-cored military unit, asshole." He seemed to be muttering to the comatose Altair as he read. "There it is! Faithfully recorded, you stupid machine. What we got here...?" Simons slowed down and started reading through the code, scrolling from the bottom up. "The lieutenant has a concussion, 1.31 minutes, yada yada yada... who would've thought an android said so much?" He scrolled further, faster.

"What's this about fucking dream fragments? And changing your skin? This what passes for flirting among androids? Fucking creepy. Hm, this looks more promising, talking to the mayor. About your cock?? Fuck's sake, this android." Simons sounded frustrated. "Come on, I'm practically back where you came aboard. There has to be something. When did you sabotage the ship?"

Marcie bit her lip, wondering what to do. Simons seemed to think that Altair had sabotaged the ship and was looking for evidence. Marcie knew he wouldn't find it, though. She looked at Altair. What were all the cables for? At least one must be responsible for Altair's lack of movement, an interruption to his synapses. She wouldn't be able to drag Altair away from Simons and to the escape pod if he were unmoving. But if she could pull the right cable, maybe he'd boot up again and move under his own power?

She traced one cable to a spot on the back of Altair's neck, and noted its colour and position hanging in the air of the room. She would have to wait for the right moment. She pulled a screwdriver from her tool belt and held it in her fist.

Then she made the mistake of looking once more at the beautiful angles of Altair's face. His eyes were open. He'd spotted her. His purple irises shone brightly, and his eyes were wide, afraid. Enraged. He knew what was happening to him, and he couldn't do anything about it. She couldn't wait anymore, couldn't leave him that way.

Marcie eased herself out of her hiding spot, reaching for the cable she thought would release Altair. But in her haste, she'd timed it poorly. Simons turned and saw her.

Marcie turned her reach for the cable into a reach for the corner of the unit to haul herself upright, trying to hide that she had a plan.

Simons started, then grinned. "Marcie, babe, you looking for me?"

Marcie made a retching sound. "As if. You know why I'm here." She held the screwdriver against the underside of her forearm, out of Simons' sight, though he could probably tell she held something.

Simons' grin took on a mocking edge. "Looking for your vibrating sex toy here? Sorry, it's not operational at the moment. You'll have to get your jollies elsewhere." He looked her up and down. "I'd offer my services, but I'm not into freaky fucks with machine fetishes." Simons had always given Marcie the heebie jeebies, but the particular twist of his face in the emergency lighting made her stomach churn. His vitriol was palpable.

"In case you hadn't noticed, the ship's going down. We have to abandon ship." Marcie reached out with a foot as she spoke, trying to catch the cable without Simons noticing.

Simons snorted. "There's a virus, right? Or you would've got the engine online again. It wouldn't've deployed a virus that it couldn't disable. Because what would be the point otherwise? The androids want our tech. Just let me get it out of him, and we can stop the ship from crashing."

"It wasn't him. You just read the transcript of his time on the ship. He didn't do anything. He didn't have time to."

"There must be something!" yelled Simons. "We can't be going down. We can't! We'll be marooned!"

"Yes, we will be. But the captain sent a mayday. We'll get rescued." Marcie caught the cable and twirled her foot, wrapping it around her ankle. She tugged. Tugged again.

Simons grabbed hold of the table and swung over it. "I have places to be, bitch. There are people who expect... Anyway, I'm not giving up on saving the ship. Not yet."

As Simons loomed closer, Marcie realised that he thought he was the hero here, that he was in the right. She wouldn't be able to make him see her logic. She tugged once more as Simons reached for her, his hand open to cover her mouth. One end of the cable freed. The other caught. Marcie couldn't back off any further; her ankle was stuck.

"Give up on it, Marcie," said Simons as he put a hand over her mouth, his shadow casting on her as his shoulders blocked her view of Altair. "You should never have had anything to do with an android that was a risk to the ship. You're the one who'll face a Court Martial, not me."

Marcie brought the screwdriver up to her shoulder. She stabbed.

Simons yelled, looked down in disbelief at the screwdriver sticking out of his shoulder. He twisted away from her, his control over his position in the room lost. Marcie too drifted back, but her ankle was still caught. She waved her leg around, trying to free herself.

"Fucking bitch!" yelled Simons. "You're a shit engineer. You only got in because your mother was hot shit. You're nothing. Nothing!"

Marcie glared at him over her shoulder as she fought to twist out of the cable. "I fixed the goddamned comms array while I had a tear in my space suit and the use of only one hand. I've kept the engine going through a punishing Weft-Skip schedule. And I explained our ship's requirements to a fucking *rainbow octopus*! I'm a great engineer, I'll have you know!"

Simons grabbed the edge of the table and swung himself into a controlled position again. He hooked one leg around the table leg, then pulled something from his belt and pointed it at Marcie. A laser gun.

"Oh, yeah?" he said. "Too bad you won't have a chance to tell Mummy you made good in the end, huh?"

Marcie gulped. She couldn't avoid it.

There was a snapping sound, a blink of movement.

A blue hand shot out towards the gun. A flash of light stunned Marcie.

CHAPTER 26

He floated in a void. Or was he the void, and something floated within him?

A voice muttered nearby, but he could not understand it.

Floating.

Steady.

Purposeless.

There must be purpose, or what is the use of existence?

ANDROID 26573-B DELETED MEMORY 5891

Flood waters. If there was one thing he could do, it was carry children through the flood waters. He was tall, steady, and strong, and the human children were so fragile. Their parents too.

Pollux was there, too, in the torrent. He also bore children on his broad red shoulders. They stood together as ever, protecting these humans, living with them as the other androids did not. Being their champions in this harsh, fledgling world.

Castor reached the edge of the flood waters and clambered onto dry ground, handing the children to their crying mothers.

Wait. This is not happening now. It happened in the past.

ANDROID 26573-B DELETED MEMORY 8004

Castor watched as the humans celebrated a birthday. They were inebriated, and he was concerned that someone would harm themselves.

A woman called Vernie sat beside him, a lascivious smile on her face, and ran her hand over his red arm. Castor looked up at Dr Neale's face. She smiled and nodded encouragingly, her mass of curly brown hair sliding over her shoulder. This was allowed. It was encouraged. After all, she would want the data.

Wait. This is not happening now either. It happened in the past.

ANDROID 26573-B DELETED MEMORY 10768

Screams. Panic. This was worse than the flood.

"We must help the humans reach the ship," said Pollux.

"Yes."

"Dr Neale confirms the *Phobos II* has sufficient shielding to protect humans from the solar flare."

"Acknowledged."

Castor gathered humans and helped them to the *Phobos II*. The elderly. The children. It was his purpose. To protect the humans. Some other androids assisted, delegated to secondary protector roles. All humans were accounted for.

All except one.

A voice. "Are all the people safely aboard?"

"All except for yourself," confirmed Castor.

"Good."

She pressed a button.

The ship exploded in flame.

Pollux ran towards the humans first.

Castor turned to the doctor. "Why would you do that?"

"Because they're corrupting the data. It has to be just you here, or it all means nothing."

Castor did not understand. He ran too.

Pollux was tearing a mangled panel from the *Phobos II* and reaching inside. Flames writhed out. Pollux reached for the people, his arms blackening. Castor ran up alongside his brother and assisted. The humans were all inside. He had to save them. To save. His hands charred, but he...

REBOOTING

ANDROID 26573-B MEMORY 1

The nameless android stood near an unknown soot-stained wreck covered in dust. His feet were ankle-deep in dirt that small dandelion plants grew in. His hands were blackened.

There were signs of hasty human evacuation all around, but there were no humans. Only androids.

Who am I?

Did I do this?

What have I done?

Come, be designated.

You are Altair, Welcome Centre Host.

I am...

Wait.

This is not happening now either. I am Altair, and I need to save Marcie before the ship crashes.

Sirens blare. Simons is shouting. He yells in pain.

Marcie's tear-streaked face, pale with shock, and yet firm with satisfied determination. She has hurt Simons. Good. But now she is drifting in zero gravity.

This is happening now. This.

Simons reached for an item on his belt. The weapon he had taken from the security officer. He pointed it at Marcie.

She could not avoid it.

Altair tore through restraints holding him down. He reached for the weapon. In the split second before he grabbed it, he saw the trigger depress under Simons' finger. Altair changed the angle of his reach and put his hand in front of the beam. The weapon discharged, and Altair's arm swung back, jolting his shoulder. The smell of singed electronics rose from him.

Altair looked down. A blue arm with a blackened hand. The sight was so much like his morning memories. But now he knew the truth. Now, as then, the blackened ruins of his skin were a badge of honour. He was an android who did his best to protect. He may have failed in the past, because Dr Neale fooled him. Simons was no Dr Neale. He was nothing.

Altair swung off the table and magnetised to the deck. He was tethered to many cables, but they had enough slack in them for him to grab Simons' weapon with one hand, and his neck with the other. Altair crushed one of these items, as much as he would have liked to crush both.

"I do not like you," he said to Simons, the blackened silicone of his fingers leaving smudges on the man's neck. "If I were another android, I might have disposed of you for attempting to kill my special person. But I would have to compromise my morals to do so, and you are not worth that much to me."

Simons' eyes were wide, and he whimpered.

"Marcie, are you all right?" asked Altair, not taking his eyes from Simons.

There was a shuffle behind him. "Yeah. I'm good. How about you?"

"Entangled, injured, and enlightened, but otherwise well."

Marcie began unclipping Altair from the cables that had been shoved through the joins in his silicone to monitoring points.

"It's still a dangerous android, Martin-Palmer," choked out Simons.

"You're the dangerous one here," said Marcie as she worked. She took the last cable off. "You're free now," she said to Altair. "Are all your processes running again?"

"I have not had the opportunity to run a full diagnostic."

Marcie put a hand on Altair's arm. "What do we do with Simons?"

Altair pondered. "I will not harm him. I will not harm a human."

"And I've already done so. Why don't we just leave him? Let's get to an escape pod. The engine could go at any moment."

Simons made a pathetic squeaking sound. "You're not going to tie me down in here? Make me go down with the ship?"

"We're not like you," said Marcie.

Altair gave Simons a shove as he let him go, sending the man careening out of control to the far end of the room. Then he took Marcie's arm and helped her to the door of the lab. Outside in the corridor, she grabbed a hold of a railing and started pulling herself along, but he took her hand with his good one and ran like he had with O'Donoghue. If the engine could explode without warning, they had no time to waste.

"Escape pods are up on fourth, the floor above us," said Marcie. "You're *limping*!"

"Let us examine the damage to my leg after we have evacuated." Sirens blared and red emergency lighting flashed as Altair ran up the stairwell, pulling Marcie with him. There were few other noises. No human feet. No voices. The other crew members had already left the ship.

At the top of the stairs, they had two choices: port or starboard.

“Let’s try port,” said Marcie, tugging on his arm.

They moved together down the hallway. Altair kept their balance in the lack of gravity, but Marcie was the one leading him to the row of angled hatches.

“No no no,” said Marcie as they ran past hatch after hatch with red indicator lights on them. “I may have chosen wrong.”

“Let us check them all on this side before we try starboard.”

Altair sped up. There, finally. At the end of the row, the final hatch had a green indicator light. Marcie tagged the door, and it slid open. Altair pushed her through the hatch and dropped in after her. Inside, there were two padded bench seats very close together with two safety harnesses on each, and a small console in front of a porthole that was currently only showing a metal panel on the other side. They had to climb over the back bench to get to the front one.

“Must we wait for two more people before launch?”

Marcie tapped the console. “No,” she said. “Only Simons and the captain are showing as aboard now. At least among crew members with life signs. There’s been a few casualties. There’s still eight pods on the starboard side. We can go. Strap in.”

Altair did so, as did Marcie. Then she tapped a few places on the console. The hatch clicked shut, and the panel in front of their capsule slid open and they launched. Stars whirled beyond the porthole, and then, with a roar, their small engine came to life. They did not need to pilot: the escape pod was automatically navigating. The planet came into view beneath. Then, moments later, there was a bright flash, and a panel of hull plating spun past.

There was no way of looking behind them, but...

"Fuck, I think that was the engine," whispered Marcie. Her face was pale, and she clung to her harness more than necessary.

Altair reached his good foot to the side and pressed it against hers. "Did your captain evacuate in time?"

"I don't know."

Their capsule spun to do a reverse burn to slow their descent. Once it did so, they could see the damage. Most of the ship was intact, but now spinning end-over-end. The engine section, Marcie's place of work, had broken off and was a cloud of debris and rapidly extinguishing inferno.

The *Sunda Tiger* would never voyage again.

CHAPTER 27

Tears beaded from Marcie's eyes and floated about the escape pod, settling against the back wall because of the burn. The *Sunda Tiger* had been her home for most of the last four years of her life. Now it was gone.

"How did this happen?" she asked in a quiet voice.

"Simons thought I sabotaged the ship. It is why he was interrogating me."

"I don't believe that for a moment. And that wasn't an interrogation. It was torture."

Altair rubbed his good foot against her ankle. "Do you think so?"

"I know so." Her anger at what she had seen roughened her words. "By the cables he had in you, he was bypassing and disrupting many of the functions in your body and mind. That must have been agonising."

Altair looked down at his blackened hand, the one he had damaged to save her life. "I was not there with him in the room most of the time. I was lost in my mind."

"Lost?"

He looked sidewards at her, his eyes glowing deep purple. "In my memories. Marcie, I remember. I remember the time before the Event Horizon and what happened."

Marcie gaped. "It's even more important that we get you safely back to the research centre, then. Sirius will need to speak to you. Won't he?" There was the possibility, after all, that Sirius was the problem.

"Yes, I need to speak to him."

Marcie tapped at the panel, double checking that their pod had the correct autopilot routine running. They were headed for the research centre, with an offset of 30 metres from buildings, people, and other escape pods.

"Can you tell me what you remembered?"

Altair rubbed her ankle again. He seemed to have decided he needed to give her reassuring contact. Or maybe he needed it. "I always suspected that I did something to the humans. But I did not. Marcie, I was a protector. I was injured trying to save them."

Marcie's tears welled up again. She could imagine how important this revelation must be for Altair. He had been afraid for so long about what lurked in his past. "That's fantastic, Altair. Not that you were injured, of course. But that you were a helper all along. I knew that was the case, but I had no evidence to convince you."

"How did you know?"

"Because you're a good person through and through, and it shows."

"That could have been programming."

"You haven't been programmed in decades. You must be exactly who you really are. There's no way it could have been faked if you were individuating."

"Thank you, Marcie."

She rubbed his ankle back. "So, what happened?"

"The head researcher of the centre. Her name was Dr Rebecca Neale. She murdered the other humans."

Marcie felt a chill at his words. "All of them?"

"Yes. She tricked us with fake data readouts and told us there was a solar flare. 227C's magnetosphere is weaker than Earth's and its primary more volatile, so solar flares can be hazardous. The humans sheltered in one particular ship, the one with the best shielding. She caused an explosion in that ship, and then programmed the other ships to leave unmanned, to obfuscate the trail."

"Why?"

"I only received part of her explanation before my mind was wiped. She said something about humans corrupting the data, and that the project would be meaningless if the data were corrupted."

"That's crazy," whispered Marcie. The thought of all of those people being murdered in such a horrific way nauseated her. "Wait, Rebecca Neale. I know that name... why do I know it?" Marcie thought she had even heard it recently. "Ah! Hellas Basin!"

"Hellas Basin?"

"The site of a tragedy that happened about 40 years ago. Some androids supposedly individuated and caused a massacre. There're a lot of conspiracy theories about what happened. I think Dr Neale was the head researcher for that project."

Altair opened his mouth to ask more, but then a gentle rushing around them turned into a roar that cut through their voices. They had entered the atmosphere, and Marcie couldn't hear him anymore.

Their descent became bumpier, and Marcie pushed her head back into the seat padding to protect her neck. Altair did the same. The orange glow of burning atmosphere lit the interior. She couldn't focus on Altair anymore because the judders of the ship blurred her vision.

Soon, a loud chime sounded, and a notification flashed up on the pod's panel. They were nearly at their destination. The engine burned hard, and a parachute extended above them. Then their momentum slackened, and they started dropping, their fall hindered only by the parachute. Marcie felt like she was lying on her back now that gravity took precedence.

"The research centre is somewhere below," she said. "The exact landing position will be offset a bit to avoid crashes and entanglements."

They lowered, and lowered, looking up at the parachute through the porthole then—

SPLASH

Water flooded over the porthole.

Marcie gaped in shock. "What?"

"We have landed in the lake," said Altair.

Why wasn't the lake offset? It should have been offset! This wasn't a floating capsule — it hadn't been installed with floatation devices! No air. No air around her. A hole in her glove.

"This is unexpected," said Altair. "We should evacuate." He unclipped his harness. "Marcie, are you all right?"

Marcie looked up at him. He kneeled on the back of his seat and leaned over her, touching her face. Her breathing was fast, and not in a good way. They had to get out. But she wouldn't be able to breathe out there. Her stomach churned.

Oh fuck, she thought. *That near-disastrous spacewalk had a bigger effect than I thought...*

"I don't feel so good."

"We have to exit the pod in case the bottom of the lake blocks our egress." As he said that, there was a small thump and a scraping noise. They listed to one side, tilting until the seats were upside down, taking Marcie with them. Worse, they were hatch-down in the mud of the lake bottom.

"Fuck, what do we do?" asked Marcie. Panic was rising in her. She was usually better than this, but after everything she'd been through in the last 24 hours, she was just about out of can-do.

Altair, who stood on the 'ceiling' now, put an arm around her shoulders and then unclipped her harness. He helped her right herself. "The situation is bothering you."

"Altair, we're trapped on the bottom of the lake! You'll be fine, but I'll run out of air."

He held her face with both of his hands, gently running his thumbs over her cheeks. "Do not panic. We have time. The oxygen content of the air is still well within your limits."

"But—"

"Is this because of the spacewalk yesterday? Did your confidence for feats like this take damage?"

Marcie bit her lip. "Maybe. Yes. I just— I don't know if I can survive a big risk like this again. It's not the same, but somehow it seems the same."

"Do you know what else is the same?"

Marcie shook her head.

"I am here. And I will not let anything happen to you. You risked your safety to save me on the ship when you did not need to. Let me do that much at least. I am an android who saves humans. I always have been."

Marcie's breath evened out. She ran a finger over his sculpted cheek bone. "You're here."

"Yes."

"We can do this together."

"Yes."

"How much oxygen do you think I have?"

"So long as the supply indicator on the control panel continues to decrease in a linear fashion, I estimate you have one hour, seven minutes of remaining air under normal conditions, and forty-three minutes of air if you were to breathe as fast as you were a minute ago."

"Good." Marcie pulled him to her and kissed him hard. He froze a moment, then responded. She deepened the kiss, ran a hand through his hair.

When she came up for breath, Altair raised an eyebrow. "Are you intending to use all the air in such a fashion? I would have thought intimate relations could wait until you were no longer in mortal peril."

"Don't worry, I only needed that kiss. Forty-three minutes isn't long enough to show you the true depth of my appreciation." She gave him a small smirk. "Now, what do we do?"

"I would like to try rocking the capsule from side to side, and using my weight to roll it over. I am very heavy, and my weight may be enough."

"Sure. I'll help, even if I don't have much mass."

They stood facing each other, their legs spread wide across the curve of the ceiling and their arms braced. "Are you ready?" asked Altair.

"Yes. Let's try to keep in rhythm. It should be easy for us. We've kept good rhythm before." She grinned and waggled her eyebrows.

He blinked, then raised an eyebrow once he had parsed her innuendo. "Agreed. Three, two, one, go." He nodded his head to his right, Marcie's left.

They began rocking side to side, pushing with their legs. The capsule rocked in the mud. Marcie wasn't sure she was having much of an effect. Altair was doing most of the work. Worryingly, his damaged leg creaked each time he pushed on it.

"Keep it up," he said. "We are gaining momentum."

The capsule was indeed rolling more to the side at each pass. On one side, it began banging against something hard. A large rock. Marcie nodded her head to the opposite side, and Altair gave a brief nod, agreeing. They stomped harder on that side, trying to tip the capsule. Something was graunching on that side: a smaller rock, perhaps. It was holding them back too, but hopefully not as much as on the other side.

They rocked harder and began to tip up onto whatever was in their way. But each time, they tipped back down onto the roof again.

"Harder," said Altair.

Marcie grabbed a harness and hefted herself up. The next time they balanced on that stone for a moment, she swung herself and kicked hard on the side of the capsule, higher than she had her foot before. They balanced on that small rock for a moment—

—a moment more—

—and they rolled down the other side. The capsule moved far enough that the hatch faced sidewards and slightly down. Altair performed the same move Marcie had and stomped the capsule along the lake bed a little more until the hatch faced fully sidewards.

"Just in case the lake mud blocked the hatch," he explained. "You will not have time to dig out of mud once the hatch is open."

Marcie gulped. "I certainly will not."

They knelt together by the hatch and were silent for a moment. "Is there anything on board the capsule that will make this escape easier for you?" asked Altair.

"No. These things aren't supposed to go in water. They're supposed to be smarter than that. I think it only happened because so many capsules were landing at the same time around a crowded settlement."

"Does the data available show how deep we are? Are you at risk of decompression illness?"

"There's no data. But I think since the air in here isn't compressed, I'll be fine. I mean, what's in my lungs will compress once I'm out there, but it will decompress again to a normal oxygen saturation. I think? Also, I still see light coming through the porthole, so we can't be that deep."

Altair blinked. "Indeed. I had not made that connection. I seem to have some holes in my data regarding oxygen behaviour."

"Makes sense if your memory was wiped to cover up humans being burned alive in a ship, right? It wouldn't have worked if you were left with the ability to piece together the evidence around you."

"Hmm." Altair put his hand on the hatch. "We should continue this line of thought later. But now, I think we should get ready for our escape. The hatch should not be a problem since it would be built to hold air in more securely than water out."

"Yes. Once we unclip it, it should swing in under the water pressure."

"Noted. I will take a deep breath of air before we go. The air will be for you, if you need it half-way."

Marcie smiled. "You'll breathe it into my mouth?"

"Yes. Is there anything else you need to prepare?"

Marcie checked her body. She shucked off her tool belt to make herself more streamlined, but her uniform was trim enough that it wouldn't drag. "How about you?" she asked. "Will the water damage your leg?"

Altair looked down at the offending, degloved limb. "Yes. But it can be repaired. Please hold on to my back while I open the hatch. We will wait a moment for the capsule to fill with water, then I will help you swim to the surface."

"OK. Give me a moment." Marcie held onto Altair's torso, gripping tight onto his t-shirt. She buried her face against his spine. "I just need a moment to prepare."

"Take your time."

She breathed in and out a few times. Flashes of her space walk came to her again, and her knees felt like jelly. But Altair was here with her. The android who saves. And she was an OK swimmer. It would be fine. "OK, give me a countdown."

"Five, four, three—"

Marcie took a deep breath, braced herself.

"—two, one."

Water blasted into the capsule. It swept Marcie's legs to the side, banging her heels on the plating. But then Altair grabbed her arms to hold her steady. Water rushed over Marcie's head. She forced her eyes open.

Altair pushed her in front of him and out of the hatch. He followed, and took hold of her around the back with one arm, swimming with the other. Marcie lost her sense of which way was up because of the sediment swirling around them, but Altair pulled her up, up. She kicked her legs, occasionally kicking his shins, and held onto his shoulder with one arm while swimming with the other.

She had no time to remember anything but how to hold her breath.

Her lungs burned. She couldn't hold her breath any longer. She lost her lung of air, and her hand spasmed on Altair's shoulder. He stopped swimming and pulled her in as if for a kiss. When Marcie needed her next breath, she put her lips to his. They lazily ascended as he blew a lungful of air into her. She smiled at him in the dappled light. Then they began swimming again.

They were ascending well. They would make it. The light was brighter and brighter.

But then something brushed against Marcie's leg. She tried to kick it away, but whatever it was twisted around her, just like the cable in the engineering lab. Her progress halted. It took Altair a moment to realise Marcie was being held back. They both looked down and saw a parachute cord caught around Marcie's calf. She shook her leg, but in her panic, couldn't shake herself free.

Altair turned in the water and moved hand-over-hand down her body to the cord. Instead of taking time to untangle it, he simply tore the strong cord apart with his hands.

Altair took hold of her again and they resumed surfacing. Marcie's lungs were burning; if only the cord hadn't stopped her. She needed more air. Altair helped her again, but far less air came her way this time. He was out. That was the last of it.

Closer, closer. Burning. It hadn't been enough. Closer. She lost her final breath.

No! Don't inhale. Don't inhale.

Darkness. Where is up? Hands on her. Legs kicking near her own. Choking down a small bit of water by accident.

Then, finally, they broke free of the surface. Marcie coughed the water out, gasped for breath. Her lungs were heaving. Rain pelted her wet hair. A warm, smooth body bobbed with her, held her close.

The piercing shriek of a bird of prey. A higher chirrup.

"We are over here!" Altair bellowed from shockingly close.

Being hefted up over plastic into the bottom of an inflatable dingy, Altair falling in beside her. Rain on her face.

"It is all right, Marcie. You are safe. You did fantastic. Rest now."

She fell into oblivion.

CHAPTER 28

The dinghy bumped into the stony shore of the lake. Elnath, Altair's fellow Welcome Centre host, jumped over the side into the shallows and dragged the dinghy ashore. Their other rescuer was Larawag, another of his fellow hosts. Altair was impressed that the dinghy had still been sound enough to inflate and perform a rescue mission. It was a remaining item from before the Event Horizon.

As soon as he felt stones through the plastic, Altair stood, scooping Marcie into his arms. Her wet uniform clung to her body, and her hair dripped onto her face. The inclement weather made sure she would have no chance to dry unless he took her inside a building.

Delichon perched on Marcie's chest, its feathers wet and ruffled, looking at her with a cocked head. The bird regularly announced Marcie's heart rate and body temperature. Altair had already sent Hieraaetus to Sirius, letting the mayor know he had returned with important information.

Marcie had remained unconscious for the duration of the dinghy trip. She had coughed up the small amount of water she had inhaled, and she was not curling up like a person experiencing decompression illness. Her breathing was even, her temperature low but not in hypothermic range, and her face placid. As far as he could tell, she had fallen unconscious because of exhaustion and relief. But her ongoing lack of consciousness concerned him.

Several more dinghies perched on the lake shore. Half a dozen other parachutes floated on the water. Theirs had not been the only escape pod to land in the lake. The hillsides beyond the town also had parachutes stuck in the treetops. Presumably, many more lay in the wide landing field.

Altair strode to the top of the dune with Marcie in his arms. The research centre beyond was a hive of activity. There were many more androids running errands than normal, and he spotted several humans in Orion Navy uniforms as well, hugging their arms around themselves and looking bedraggled in the rain. They were gathering together and walking towards the central square.

"We have opened the medical centre," said Larawag from behind Altair. "Many humans have sustained injuries. The humans who do not require medical attention are gathering beyond the town in the landing field. We do not know why they will not come into the research centre unless necessary. We have given them tents to shelter them against the rain, but we opened the town hall as well, in case they change their minds."

"They are still unsure about us," said Altair. "We will need to work hard to earn their trust. I will take Marcie to the medical centre. Her status concerns me." Waiting no longer, Altair strode through the town. His leg creaked with each step, and the range of movement in his ankle seemed limited, but his treatment could wait.

Outside the building, Altair found two humans supporting another one who was favouring their leg even more than Altair was. The trio stood by the door as if unsure whether they should enter.

"Please follow me," said Altair as he walked past them to the double doors.

"Is she OK?" one human asked.

"I do not yet know. We swam out of our escape pod." Altair carried Marcie through the lobby and into the treatment area beyond. A dozen androids bustled around the room, putting out supplies, rolling out beds, and setting up a triage area. Several humans worked among them, perhaps the *Sunda Tiger's* medical staff. All the humans attended patients, of which there were already a dozen. The androids who attended to humans treated the unconscious ones. Perhaps the humans who were conscious had objected to being treated by androids.

Altair was relieved to see Lieutenant O'Donoghue in a bed, one of the medical humans shining a light into his eyes. The man was joking with the person treating him, so presumably the injury to his head was not serious.

Altair took Marcie to one of the unoccupied beds. Naos, a dark blue female-shaped android designated as a medical android, walked over to them. "Who is the patient, and what is the problem?"

"This is Lieutenant Marcie Martin-Palmer. Our escape pod landed in the lake. She fell unconscious and has remained so ever since we swam out of the pod and boarded a dinghy."

"Your human, then."

Delichon then spoke. "Heart rate is 56 beats per minute. Temperature is 35.4°C."

"Concerning," said Naos. "Undress her."

"Undress her?"

"Cold, wet clothing is hazardous to humans."

Altair unzipped Marcie's uniform and rolled her to one side and then the other so he could peel it off. Delichon flew above the bed while he did so, then resettled. Marcie's lips and fingernails looked blue. Naos brought over a stack of musty yet warmed blankets and started laying them over Marcie. Altair helped with that too. Then Naos wheeled over a monitoring machine and hooked Marcie up to it. The machine beeped steadily.

"She is cold and exhausted, and has suffered minor bruising," said Naos. "But she will recover. She will wake in a few hours. I will provide intravenous fluids and nutrients to speed up her recovery. Thank you for bringing in the patient. You may leave."

Altair did not want to leave. He wanted to stay and wait until Marcie regained consciousness. She looked so small and fragile under the layers of blankets. The old bruise on her cheekbone had faded to a pale yellow smudge, but new ones dotted her limbs.

Naos noted Altair's hesitation. "You will be needed elsewhere, Altair. We will take care of her."

Just then, three more people entered the medical centre: Marcie's work mates Chaudhary and Kikelomo, who between them supported the security officer Simons had attacked. They took the officer to a bed, then Chaudhary spotted Marcie.

The two of them rushed to Marcie's bedside. "Is she OK?" asked Kikelomo.

"I do not know," said Altair. "We landed in the lake."

"She will recover," said Naos. She began explaining Marcie's condition to her friends. They listened and gave Altair glances he could not parse.

Altair looked up at the door as it opened again. Then he stood straight. The humans picked up on his attention, because they looked too.

In the doorway stood Captain Rodriguez, a wound on her lip and a weapon in her hand, and in front of her a worse-for-wear Simons. The screwdriver wound Marcie inflicted had bled down the front of his uniform, and his face was dirty and twisted with unpleasant emotions.

"This one needs both medical attention and restraints," said Captain Rodriguez. "What can we do, people?"

The whole room watched the proceedings. One of the medical androids ushered them to a bed and then produced a pair of handcuffs. "We can treat him here and cuff him to the bed."

"I did nothing wrong!" yelled Simons. "You all have it in for me, you freaks!"

Naos had been right that Altair would be needed. He stroked Marcie's cold cheek, gave her friends a nod, and approached the bed they were trying to get Simons into. "Captain, if I may?"

Captain Rodriguez turned and looked him up and down, then looked beyond him to where Marcie lay. "Is she OK?"

"I have been assured she will be."

The captain nodded. "Good. What do you have to say?"

Altair made sure his voice carried to the entire room. "Simons is telling a falsehood when he says he did nothing."

"We all know about the mess hall incident, Altair."

"I am not referring to that, captain. Simons attacked that security officer there," he pointed. "Then he tried to hack me. When Marcie came to my aid, he tried to shoot her."

"I was trying to figure out how you'd sabotaged the ship! And I didn't shoot at Martin-Palmer!"

Altair held his blackened hand up. "I blocked the shot myself, as you can see." There were gasps behind him. "And I did not sabotage the ship, a fact you uncovered quickly in my data. But you kept looking." Altair stared at the twisted face of the head engineer. This man had violated him. It was not the worst violation he had ever experienced, but it had been distinctly unpleasant, nonetheless.

Captain Rodriguez looked at him for a long moment, then took the handcuffs. "Let's get him restrained."

Altair stepped forward.

"You can't push me around!" yelled Simons. Altair picked the man up with ease and pushed him down onto the hospital bed. He used perhaps a bit more force than necessary. Simons looked at him with fear. Had the man only just realised how much stronger than him Altair must be?

The captain cuffed the man to the bed's railing. "Treat him, but do not let him escape or bother others, if you please. Sedate him if necessary."

"Understood," said the assisting medical android.

The captain looked up at Altair. "Would you be so kind as to take me to Sirius, please? I suspect we both need to have an urgent word with him."

Altair gave Marcie one last look. Her friends and Naos were still attending to her. "Please, this way, captain."

Androids watched them warily as they cut a diagonal across the square to the Mayor's Office. The rain was letting up. Altair's clothes were still wet, though, and he made squelching noises along with the creaking of his leg. Perhaps he could take the clothes off again now that he was home. But now, right in front of the humans' captain, was not the time.

He led the captain inside. Sirius was standing in the corridor, conferring with Pollux. No, Vega. Now that Altair had memories from before the Event Horizon, they were interfering with his more up-to-date knowledge. Vega did not know it, but he and Altair had once considered themselves to be brothers. That familial relationship was erased in the Event Horizon. Ever since, Altair had not been comfortable around Vega because of his incorrect suspicions about the role they had played in the disappearance of the humans. Dr Neale had stolen much more from them than he had at first suspected.

While Altair pondered, Sirius noted their approach. "Keep watch but do not antagonise our human guests," Sirius said to Vega.

"Understood." Vega turned to leave. He paused a moment, looking at Altair. More specifically, at Altair's blackened hand. Vega too had damaged his hands trying to save the humans before the Event Horizon, and likely too had lingering concerns.

As Vega moved to pass them in the corridor, Altair grabbed his forearm. "We sustained injuries before the Event Horizon trying to help the humans. That is what these wounds mean: that we are helpers."

Vega gave Altair an inscrutable look. For the 14,108th time, Altair wished he were networked with his fellows so he could know what they were thinking. He should ask, but the words would not come. Vega gave a curt nod and continued on his way.

"I was just about to send Canicula to find both of you," said Sirius, naming his familiar. "We have much to discuss. Please, come in."

They took seats in Sirius's office. The captain looked around at the glass furniture, the silver sheer curtains, the electrofilm windows with the view of the lake and the scudding clouds above.

Sirius shut the door. Canicula, a black retriever-type dog android, sat on a dog bed in the corner, the blue light of a recharge cycle in its eyes.

"I have received conflicting reports of what happened," said Sirius. "Can you give further detail?"

"First, one of our runabouts, the one our landing party used, exploded in our hangar bay," said Captain Rodriguez. "It was sabotaged. Then, when we attempted to assess the damage and get the *Sunda Tiger* back under control, we found a nasty virus in our computer systems. Our engineers couldn't regain control, and we were forced to abandon ship."

"Do you think we were responsible?" asked Sirius.

"I think we were supposed to think that," said the captain. "That was the implication of the situation. However, we had a stroke of luck." She took a moment to brush at some smudges on her uniform. A futile effort, as she must have crossed some rugged terrain after disembarking from her escape pod. There were twigs in her hair and mud caked down one side. "Lieutenant Martin-Palmer, who was a part of the landing party—"

Both the captain and Sirius glanced at Altair.

"—she didn't like the sound of the runabout when it returned to the *Sunda Tiger*. She lodged a maintenance request. Shortly before the explosion, I received a report from one of our mechanics. She found evidence that we had a stowaway."

"A stowaway? Of what kind?" asked Sirius.

"The mechanic found some items in an overhead storage compartment that were crumpled, ran a diagnostic, and found evidence of unknown DNA. Human DNA."

"A human who is not a part of your crew was aboard?" asked Altair.

"Yes. There was no footage of any intruders aboard, but there were a few incidences of doors opening for no visible reason. I believe we had an intruder who had cloaking technology beyond what the Orion Navy currently has, who sabotaged the ship. There were no unexplained door openings after we ferried Sirius back to the surface, so we think the intruder stowed away again for that journey as well. The runabout that was used for that trip will have been destroyed so we can't check it for evidence."

"Did you have time to compare the DNA sample with a larger database than your own crew, captain?" asked Altair.

"No. We're hoping that we'll be able to salvage some of our ship, and perhaps if we're lucky, we'll have a working computer. We'll check then if we can. I have a copy of the sample readout."

"If you can run that check, start by comparing the sample with one Dr Rebecca Neale."

"Who is that?" asked Sirius.

But Captain Rodriguez's eyes widened. "I know who that is. She was in charge of the Hellas Android Research Centre. She was missing, presumed dead after the Hellas massacre."

"Yes. I believe she was in charge of Research Centre 227C. My memories indicate she was responsible for the murder of the other human colonists. And that she survived the Event Horizon."

Altair outlined for them how Simons had tried to hack him, and had uncovered hidden memories within his databanks. He also pieced together what he had remembered. The captain winced as he told the story of the fire.

"Therefore, I suspect Dr Neale may still be monitoring her experiments, that is to say us, while cloaked so we cannot detect her. She is a prime candidate for the stowaway aboard the runabout."

"Interesting," said the captain. "I'll keep that in mind. If so, this research centre was an illicit one, I'm sorry to say. No one else would have allowed Dr Neale to run another set of android experiments."

"This all seems far-fetched," said Sirius. "If this is true, then we have spent nearly three decades not noticing a human living nearby and observing us. Would we not have seen some sign?"

"What about the ping to the Welcome Centre security system from the other night? Could that have been her?" asked Altair.

"What ping?" asked Sirius.

"The one I reported to you and Vega."

"I received no report. I have the security readouts from the Welcome Centre here. I reviewed them. There was nothing of note."

"Yes, you did receive a report. And it should have been in the readout too. I received a notification while recharging one night."

The captain frowned. "What if you have been seeing evidence of an observer all along, but she periodically wipes the evidence of her existence from you? And this time, Altair remembers because he was aboard the *Sunda Tiger* during the last wipe sequence?"

"How would that be achieved when we are not networked?"

They all looked to where Canicula was charging. "I have never considered the security flaw of the recharge stations," said Sirius.

"Because we were not supposed to," said Altair. "We were programmed not to think of it."

"We cannot avoid charging."

"No. But we can rely on our human guests to remind us of what we have forgotten."

Sirius looked at the captain. "I do not think most of the humans are ready to be close to us yet. Captain, may I ask a favour of you? Please lend us Lieutenant Martin-Palmer. Considering the bond she has forged with Altair..."

"Yes. We all know about that. But that dove-tails neatly with what I was about to suggest. Altair, do you think Martin-Palmer saw enough of what Simons did to you that triggered the release of your memories to try to replicate it less uncomfortably?"

"Yes, I think so."

"I was going to suggest assigning Martin-Palmer to you to help uncover your memories. All of your memories. We need you all remembering what happened, because you all would have had unique experiences. We can't rely on Altair's memories alone."

"That is an excellent idea," said Sirius. "And if she stays close to Altair while she does so, she may observe inconsistencies in his memory too."

"Exactly. Would you mind hosting Martin-Palmer a little longer, Altair?" asked the captain.

He thought of having Marcie staying with him even longer. Maybe even for a while. The thought was a pleasant one. "It would be my pleasure."

"We know, unfortunately," said Sirius in a quiet voice. "That is decided. Captain, I wish to discuss the practicalities of how we set up accommodation for your crew and provide necessary supplies. Altair, please report to the android repair centre. The damage to your body concerns me. I will come to you for a full debrief later."

"Yes, Sirius, captain." Altair rose. "What about the investigation of what happened to the ship?"

"Oh, we will get to that, Altair," said the captain. "I assure you. We will uncover what happened."

CHAPTER 29

Outside the tent, the camp was a bustle of activity in the afternoon air. Marcie hadn't been awake for long. She'd slept the day through in the medical centre before being discharged. Marcie sat on a dining chair, of all things: the androids were bringing over an assorted collection of furniture and blankets from their settlement, anything that they could spare. Marcie thought it would be more comfortable for them to live in the settlement — the Welcome Centre alone could house scores of people at a push. But the others didn't yet seem comfortable with that idea. For now, they were establishing a temporary camp on the airfield, one with a perimeter and a roster of guards. And mud. So much mud.

Beside Marcie sat Ife, and across from them, Captain Rodriguez. Normally, the commander would have been at the captain's right hand, but Commander Mori was looking after her spouse. About a dozen crew members were suffering the effects of 227C's gravity because they were from lower gravity colonies, and Specialist Mori was one of those, as they were from Mars. It was poor luck for all of them, because they would need Specialist Mori's expertise to get food sources up and running.

"I wanted to talk to you about the engineering staff," said the captain. "We're going to need a lot from your team. But with Simons under disciplinary action, he can't lead. And a few other members of your team will need some recovery time from their injuries, so there will be some scheduling challenges."

"Marcie can step up, I'm sure of it," said Ife. "She's been a great 2IC."

Marcie smiled at her friend. Even though Marcie hadn't been able to solve the problem of the engine, her friend still supported her. That meant a lot. Even so, she didn't agree with her friend's opinion.

"Excuse me, captain. I think Ife would make a better head engineer than I would. She has the people and management skills, not just engineering skills."

Ife scoffed, but Marcie pretended she didn't hear it.

"I concur, though I think you're selling yourself short, lieutenant. The reason I agree is that we're going to be a body down semi-permanently, and that body is you, Martin-Palmer."

"Captain?"

"You have a new assignment, one that is top priority. But first: Lieutenant Kikelomo: do you think you could keep Simons in order? Because we can't lose his engineering expertise if Martin-Palmer is busy elsewhere." The captain must have seen the shock and discomfort in their faces, because she sighed. "I know: I wouldn't ask this of you under any other circumstances. He should be in a brig. But with everything going on, we're going to need his hands on the job. I'll give you the use of a dedicated security officer to keep the peace. But can you work with him? Keep him in line?"

Ife's eyebrows rose. "Oh, captain. Absolutely." There was real relish in her voice, as if she was looking forward to it.

"Then, in that case, Lieutenant *Commander* Kikelomo, I would like to appoint you as the new head engineer. I warn you: it's going to be a tough job. You'll need to lead the salvage of the *Sunda Tiger* and reconstruct what tech we can. We got a distress call out along the subspace comms before we lost the ship, but we don't know how long it'll take them to get a rescue ship out to us. We're going to need to come up with a lot of different tech solutions. Will you accept the job?"

Ife glowed, and her spine straightened. "Yes, captain. I would be honoured." She grinned at Marcie, who grinned back. What a great call! Ife was often the one keeping on top of things in engineering, making the snap decisions. Honestly, Ife should have been 2IC all along. She would be an excellent head engineer.

"What will Marcie be doing?" asked Ife. "What am I losing her to?"

"Martin-Palmer has some information that will help to uncover the androids' missing memories. We need the androids to remember what happened, so we can figure out who is threatening us now and where they are. You've been briefed about the intruder?"

Both Marcie and Ife nodded.

"Yes, well. Uncovering what happened to the androids is of utmost importance, second only to making sure our people have food in their bellies and roofs over their heads. Martin-Palmer, your presence has been requested in the settlement. Sirius has suggested that Altair could continue looking after you for a while."

"Mhmmm," said Ife.

The captain smirked. “Exact arrangements to be determined between the two of you, of course. Please report to the android settlement today or first thing tomorrow, at your convenience. Also, there is something else you’ll need to monitor. It seems whoever altered the memories of the androids has continued to do so on an ongoing basis to hide their presence. Sirius would like you to keep an eye on Altair and see if there are any inconsistencies in what he experiences and remembers. He knows you’ll be doing this, so it’s not a secret.”

“Alterations to their memories, captain?” asked Marcie. That didn’t sound good.

“I met with Sirius and Altair. We discovered that Altair’s memories of the last few days don’t align with the memories of the other androids, presumably because he was on the *Sunda Tiger* last time their memories were altered. You can ask him about the details. So: do you think you can do it? Get stuck in with uncovering their memories?”

“Yes, captain. I can.”

Ife hugged Marcie outside the tent after their meeting. “If you have any trouble over there, come back to us. I’ll support you. Same goes if anyone over here gives you grief for spending time with the androids.”

“Thank you.” It wasn’t as if she was going far. She would see everyone often. But she knew that this assignment, after the revelations in the mess hall, would put a divide between her and the rest of the crew. It meant a lot that Ife was promising to bridge that divide when needed.

“Let me know if you need me to come back to help with the bigger jobs. I’m sure I’ll be able to multi-task.”

“I will.”

Thinking of the mess hall made Marcie aware that all she’d eaten since her last meal on the *Sunda Tiger* was a chewy old energy bar at the medical centre. She decided to grab a meal at the mess tent before going to the android settlement.

Several long tables and an assortment of chairs had been set up in a large tent, along with a row of large pots of communal food donated by the androids. It was the unidentifiable gloop that Marcie had avoided eating at the Welcome Centre. If any salad makings had arrived from the Welcome Centre garden, they were long gone.

Marcie snuck around the edge of the tent to the pots and dished herself a small bowl of gloop. There were a handful of people eating at the tables, none of which were her friends. Marcie wasn't ashamed of her actions, but in amongst the rush and the danger of the previous evening, she'd never gauged how the crew thought about her after some time to reflect. Had Simons caused irreparable harm to her reputation? Or had people found a more moderate opinion of her relations with Altair after some time to consider, and after being reminded (rather forcefully) that there were more important things to worry about? Marcie wanted to just quickly fill her belly and be on her way, and then figure out her standing at leisure another day.

The nearby hubbub of conversation quietened down when Marcie took a seat at an unoccupied table. A prickle running along her arms told her she was the object of scrutiny of the group, but she just kept her head down and applied herself to her meal. She wouldn't give anyone the satisfaction of looking bothered about it. Not after the night before. She never wanted to feel that vulnerable again.

But no one said anything to her, or called her any names. They said nothing nice to her, either. Oh well. Ife still had her back, if no one else did.

Just then, another figure entered the tent. Marcie looked up and then smiled. "Sandeep! Good afternoon!"

She knew it would feel like morning to most people there because it was morning according to ship time. But the ship was no more, and they would have to get used to the time change.

Sandeep took the seat across from her. "Marcie! I heard you were up and about. Are you feeling all right? You gave us all a scare." His dark eyes were concerned.

"I'm fine now. I just needed to warm up and rest, is all."

"I've heard about your reassignment."

Marcie nodded. "I'm sorry I won't be able to help as much with the salvage."

Sandeep tilted his head and shrugged. "It's all right. What you'll be doing is important too." He leaned to the side a bit to look past her and raised his voice. "All of us among the crew understand the situation has changed and a good working relationship with the androids is essential. Right?" He looked back at her and huffed. "At least they should."

Marcie reached across the table and gripped his hand. "Thanks, Sandeep." She hoped he knew she meant not only for sticking up for her now, but also in the mess hall the night before. His support meant a lot to her.

He squeezed her hand back. "It's all right." He let go and sat further back in the chair. "Are you heading over to the settlement soon?"

"Yes."

"Check in on O'Donoghue while you're there, if you can. I think he's still at the medical centre. Bad concussion."

"I will. Though Simons is still there too. Puncture wound in his shoulder." Marcie gave a feral grin.

"Wonder how that got there."

"Who knows?" They both laughed. "Hey, you look out for Lieutenant *Commander* Kikelomo, huh? She's gonna have one hell of a job to do."

"On it. I just know she's going to forget meals. I'll make sure she gets them."

"Thanks. You know, you'll make a wonderful wife for someone one day."

Sandeep pulled the finger at Marcie, and they both laughed again.

Marcie finished her gloop and rose to put her bowl and spoon in the wash bucket. "I'd better get going before I lose the light," she said. "If you need any help getting stuff from the androids, let me know. I think I'm on the Quartermaster's good side, so I can put in a good word."

"Thanks, Marcie. Best of luck!"

With that, Marcie left the mess tent, and then the encampment. Most people may have been giving her wary looks, unsure of what to think. But her friends still stood by her, and that's all that mattered.

CHAPTER 30

Altair had been lying on a worktable in the android repair centre for 6 hours and 37 minutes. The damage to his body had been extensive. Shaula was efficient; the repair had not taken all of those hours. But she was busy attending to requests related to the human crew, and so she only occasionally had time to spare for Altair.

She had replaced parts in his leg and hand, and had run a full diagnostic of his systems. Shaula knew about the discrepancy between his memories and the memories of the androids who remained on 227C. Presumably the diagnostic was to investigate the discrepancy.

Several hours earlier, Sirius had visited and asked Shaula to leave the lab for a few minutes so that he could 'debrief Altair' about his mission. Altair had made it clear that Captain Rodriguez had been forthright about the situation, Altair did not have anything substantial to add, and that he had not liked being asked to spy.

"The only thing I can offer is that I suspect Simons' motivations are his own and nothing to do with the Orion Navy. Neither did they have anything to do with the mystery of our colony. He was not working with anyone else, and he held the mistaken belief that I was the saboteur. I believe he will continue to think that, and we will need to remain vigilant against mistaken human impressions."

Sirius had accepted Altair's debrief, and left to attend to other matters.

Now Altair lay as framework and workings upon the table, and hoped that Marcie would not come looking for him just yet. He did not know how she would react to seeing him without his skin. Shaula was preparing a new set of skin for him, adding his dimensions and attributes, such as his fingerprints, to the template before pressing it out in the machine. Altair had considered choosing a new colour, after all. But Marcie had expressed a fondness for his sky blue colour, so he kept it.

The door swooshed open, revealing Vega, who walked straight up to Altair's bedside. "You said that we are androids who save. What do you mean?" he asked without preamble.

"Before the Event Horizon, we were a matched pair of android guards who looked after the first colonists. It was our purpose to take care of them, even if we were in danger. Our hands were damaged during the Event Horizon because we tried to save the humans from a fire."

"How did you discover this? Has Sirius been keeping this information from the colony?"

There were Vega's vague suspicions again. Altair did not want to disclose his relations with Marcie to Vega, so he told the other half of the story instead. "No. A bad human amongst the crew of the *Sunda Tiger* tried to hack me before the ship crashed. His hacking attempt dislodged locked memories."

Behind him somewhere, Shaula moved restlessly. For the 14,116th time, Altair wished he was networked with his fellow androids, because he wished to know if Shaula knew the rest of the story.

"Is this human the one who is in custody at the medical centre?"

"Yes."

"Understood. I will keep a closer eye on anything to do with that particular human."

Vega turned to leave, but Altair grabbed his arm. Vega looked down at him.

"We were brothers. Before the Event Horizon. We were brothers, known as Castor and Pollux. It is why we resemble each other so much. We were made together. That is what was stolen from us in the Event Horizon."

"I do not remember," said Vega. He walked away and out the door without a backwards glance.

For the 14,117th time, Altair wished he was still networked with his fellow androids. Maybe then he would still have a connection with his brother.

Shaula approached Altair's bedside, a swathe of sky blue skin held in her own emerald hands. "You did not tell him about how you started having memories," she observed.

"He does not need to know details like that."

"Then your fraternity really is severed. If you had that kind of relationship with him, he would have been the one android you could have felt comfortable discussing it with."

She was right. There was no point in thinking about what Vega had once been to him. That was the main defining feature of an Event Horizon: what was on the other side was forever out of reach.

Shaula began affixing the skin to Altair's leg.

"What do you think of recent events?" asked Altair. After all, Marcie had reminded him that if he wanted to know what his fellow androids were thinking, all he had to do was ask.

Shaula kept working. For a moment, Altair thought she may ignore the question. But then she spoke. "The mysteries of our colony have concerned me for a long time. It has frustrated me that I could not reach any firm conclusions or uncover the truth. The discovery that our memories are being tampered with is concerning, but also vindicating. It seems I never reached the end of my investigation because someone did not want me to." She moved away to fetch another swathe of skin.

"How do you think the humans will affect the situation?"

"Humans are hard to predict. But yours took care of you when you were on her ship. She has uncovered clues. If you take responsibility for her within my lab, then I will be willing to work with her. An unhackable brain with relevant technical expertise will be useful. So long as she does not work against us."

"She will not. She will help us. I promise."

"I hope for all our sakes that you are right."

CHAPTER 31

Delichon swooped down from the sky to land on Marcie's shoulder as she left the medical centre after checking in on a groggy but recovering Faolán. "Do you know where Altair is?" she asked the bird.

"Altair is in the android repair centre," chirped Delichon.

When she approached the desk, instead of being turned away, she was waved into the centre proper. Marcie stepped through double doors into a large, white, pristine room full of machinery of all kinds, many cabinets filled with boxes of parts, and three treatment beds. Altair, naked again, reclined on one of those beds, and the green android Shaula leaned over his head from above, combing through his hair. She had her forest green hair tied back in a bun and a pen-shaped tool balanced over one ear that was pointed like an elf's. She wore an apron over her front, but nothing underneath, as expected of an android in this odd settlement. Her toned-looking arse was displayed to the room without a single hint of shame.

Altair's leg and arm looked as good as new. His hair was longer than it had been before. Dark blue strands brushed his forehead, and the back was shaggy enough to splay on the pillow. The short back and sides were gone. Looking closer, Marcie saw Shaula was rooting hairs into his scalp with a pair of small tools. One small section at his right temple was still unrooted.

"Marcie, have you recovered?" Altair asked when he spotted her.

"Yes, I'm fine. You?"

"Nearly done, I think. Shaula has replaced my entire epidermis. Much was damaged, and the rest was brittle. She is now rerooting hair."

"It's longer."

"Yes. Meeting you humans made me aware that our gender expressions were too rigid, and there was no need for me to retain one certain style just because that is what I started out with."

"I have finished," said Shaula.

Altair sat up and felt at his hair. "What do you think?"

His new style worked well with the angles of his face, accentuating his cheek bones and making his eyes seem mysterious. He looked even more like a model. "Wonderful," she said. "I like it."

"Lieutenant Martin-Palmer, you have discovered you now have access to my lab," said Shaula. "I understand we will be working together on investigating android memories and what happened before the Event Horizon."

Marcie hadn't known that she would work with Shaula specifically, but it made sense. "Yes, I believe so."

"Let us have a meeting tomorrow. I will send Charm to schedule a time. Please rest for now. I heard you have had a harrowing few days."

"I have. Thank you. See you later."

To Marcie's surprise, while she chatted, Altair put the clothes he had been assigned on the *Sunda Tiger* back on. They were grubby from the crazy night and morning, but so was her own uniform.

They stepped out together into a glorious coral sunset. Marcie yawned. "I'm sorry. I don't know why I'm so tired. I haven't been awake long."

"Shall we go to the Welcome Centre? I will make you a beverage." He led her back to the very apartment she had stayed in before. His apartment. There was a mystery box on the table. Altair put the kettle on, then opened the box. "It is clothing," he said. "While I was away, the Quartermaster turned the rayon plant on and programmed some textile bots to make clothing. They must have expected that some androids would be curious. Natural fibres will take some months to begin production." Altair lifted a basic blue shift dress out of the box. "I do not expect this is for me."

Marcie blushed. "Everyone knows I'll be here with you, don't they? *Everyone*." She took the dress and held it up against herself. It would be a bit big on her, but at least it wasn't her dirty uniform. "I'm going to take a quick shower, if that's all right. I feel gross, and I can't just get a new skin put on when I'm looking worse for wear."

She showered quickly. When she walked back into the main room, she found Altair sitting at the table wearing a basic white t-shirt, one that didn't need to stretch so much over his muscles as the black one he wore before, and basic pull-on shapeless blue trousers. Marcie figured some bright spark would give the androids better clothing patterns in time, and cotton or linen would be better than rayon. But for now, the basic clothes were much appreciated.

Altair nudged a cup of tea towards the seat across from him. Marcie took the seat and a sip of her drink.

"So," she said.

"So."

"We've got our work cut out for us, eh?"

"Indeed. A disaster, a saboteur, hacking, interpersonal conflict, an engineering challenge..."

"Everyone looking at us and wondering what we're up to..."

"We will overcome it all. Because you are here. If I am an android who saves, you are a human who solves problems."

Marcie flushed. "I hope I'm up to it."

"You are."

Marcie cleared her throat. "And is it OK if I stay here for now?"

"Please stay as long as you like. I have only known you for a few days, Marcie Martin-Palmer. But already, you have dispelled a deep well of loneliness within me I did not recognise was there, because I had not believed I had emotions until you observed them. Your presence here is more than welcome."

Marcie stood and walked around the table. She sat sidewards on Altair's lap and ran fingers through his hair, enjoying the new length. "Thank you. No one has ever met me and seen me the way you do. I always have to fight to be taken seriously. But you immediately saw me for who I am, not what I appear to be. I don't know how long we'll be here before a rescue ship comes. But I know I want to spend the time that I have here getting to know you. If that's OK."

Altair stroked her cheek. "I am looking forward to it."

Marcie placed her hands on Altair's cheeks and drew him in for a scorching kiss. His skin had a 'new transport' kind of smell that would no doubt dissipate soon. He felt as good as ever, though. She ran her hands down his shoulders, over the curves of his muscles...

Delichon flew through the electrofilm window and landed on the table, its claws scrabbling. "Marcie, you have been summoned to Mayor Sirius's office for a debrief. Please report to the mayor's office at your earliest convenience."

Marcie sighed. "Duty calls. Shall we continue this later?"

Altair gave her one more brief kiss. "I am hoping so. Go win over more androids with your charm. I will make sure there is a meal ready for you when you return."

Marcie grinned. Her life had been thrown upside down over the last week, to be sure. But the new configuration it was falling into — it looked pretty good.

To be continued...

ACKNOWLEDGEMENTS

Sometimes it feels like this book brought itself into being without effort. I don't know why, but Marcie and Altair *really* wanted their story to be told, and much of the first draft of this book appeared before I meant to start writing. But of course, it's never the case that books just 'appear'. Not all the effort was mine, either. I am thankful to my beta readers Kim and Rain, and to my long-suffering husband who alpha read the book before them. While he's not a romance reader, he is an engineer, so his advice was invaluable.

I am also, as ever, grateful to my online writing friends. I'm not sure I would even stay on track with my writing without a community of like-minded people to talk to along the way. You're all gems.

AUTHOR'S NOTE

In the world I have created for this book, the Orion Navy has a policy of naming ships after extinct species, in memoriam. However, in the real world, it is not yet too late to save the Sunda tiger, also known as the Sumatran tiger. Similar to the orangutan, the Sunda tiger is under extreme threat in its last remaining habitat, the forests of Sumatra, Indonesia.

To mark the publication of this book, I have made a donation to the International Tiger Project, an organisation that works to protect the habitat of the Sunda tiger. I recommend checking out their work. The organisation is open about how their funds are used, and has comprehensive impact reports and financial audits available on their website, which you can find at internationaltigerproject.org

ABOUT THE AUTHOR

Calanthe is a writer from Aotearoa New Zealand. She lives with her family and a very fluffy cat. She likes growing food more than flowers. She enjoys cooking and baking, and she watches K-dramas and Star Wars. By day, she is a parent and freelance editor.

Calanthe is a pākehā (white settler) who lives and works on the ancestral lands of the Kāi Tahu iwi.

Find out more at www.CalantheColt.com

www.ingramcontent.com/pod-product-compliance
Lightning Source LLC
Chambersburg PA
CBHW031943240626
47153CB00003B/838

9780473703936